Hell Bound for Spindriff

When outlaw Denny Blake betrayed the Arizona Raiders during a bank robbery in the town of Spindriff, he little realized the storm he would unleash. Sentenced to twenty years in Arizona's notorious Yuma prison, gang leader Smokin' Joe McCabe has vowed to kill Blake and burn the town to the ground, renaming it Hellfire.

Escaping after only two years, McCabe puts together a new gang and heads for Spindriff. On the trail he encounters another prodigal who has run foul of the town's spineless officials. Red Spot Rick Norton has his own reasons for seeking vengeance, and refuses to join up with McCabe. A clash between right and wrong is inevitable. But who will emerge victorious? Harsh accusations and hot lead will fly thick and fast before the final showdown.

Hell Bound for Spindriff

Dale Graham

A Black Horse Western

ROBERT HALE

© Dale Graham 2017
First published in Great Britain 2017

ISBN 978-0-7198-2497-5

The Crowood Press
The Stable Block
Crowood Lane
Ramsbury
Marlborough
Wiltshire SN8 2HR

www.bhwesterns.com

Robert Hale is an imprint
of The Crowood Press

Typeset by
Derek Doyle & Associates, Shaw Heath
Printed and bound in Great Britain by
CPI Group (UK) Ltd, Croydon, CR0 4YY

CHAPTER ONE

TRIAL AND TRIBULATION

Judge Henry Askew slammed his gavel down. The abrupt crack immediately hushed the throb of excitement that rippled around the courtroom as the venerable holder of that noble office made his solemn announcement.

'The jury will now retire to consider its verdict.'

The courtroom was packed to capacity. So full in fact that folks were even peering in through the windows to get a peak at the notorious villain on trial. It wasn't every day that a town the size of Spindriff attracted such high-profile interest. That said, the town officials sitting stiffly in their padded seats would readily have welcomed more salubrious attention. The newspaper headlines likely to be generated by the trial might well catch the fancy of unwanted n'er-do-wells and ruffians.

An hour had passed since the final summing up by the two attorneys. It seemed more like five. The steady tick of the wall clock sounded like a harbinger of doom for the man sitting in the dock. But it might not be all bad, the defendant mused hopefully.

If'n his lawyer had been sufficiently persuasive, the robber could be out soon, free as a bird. His argument that the real outlaw boss had escaped and his client was a mere passerby who had panicked when challenged had been convincingly presented. A case of mistaken identity. It had certainly caught the attention of the jury.

The heaving throng was once again buzzing with expectation.

Speculation as to the result gripped the packed audience. It wouldn't be long now. The accused, bank robber Smokin' Joe McCabe, had possessed a slick tongue when questioned by the prosecuting attorney. And backed up by an even craftier defence lawyer, the outcome was now in the hands of the twelve good men and true. Which way would they be swayed?

Yet right from the start, McCabe had not helped his case when he initially entered the dock with a cigar stuck between his teeth. The judge had ordered him to remove the trademark fixture forthwith, which did nothing for his prospects with the stern-faced official. 'Give me a break, judge, it helps a fella think straight,' McCabe clamoured, gnawing at the brown tube. 'I feel kinda naked without it.' But the plea fell on deaf ears.

All that McCabe could do now was direct his ugly grimaces at the one man who had occasioned the failure of what was meant to have been a simple bank job. He would dearly have loved to have jumped out of his seat and throttled the object of his fury. But a ball and chain firmly secured him to the heavy seat, and along with hand manacles, they effectively prevented any such action.

Sitting on the far side of the court, back stiff as a poker, the man who had double-crossed him was sweating buckets. Until his betrayal, Denny Blake had been a leading member of the McCabe Gang. Notorious throughout the territory they had been labelled the Arizona Raiders. And it was Blake who had turned States Evidence by shopping the gang's intentions to the law whilst on a scouting foray.

The reward of two thousand dollars spotted on a noticeboard for the apprehension of the gang's leader Joe McCabe was too much of a temptation. He had also managed to negotiate the job of town marshal when the existing incumbent retired in three months' time. Helping the current marshal capture a band of renegade Apaches who had been stealing cattle certainly helped swing opinion his way.

All in all, it ought to have been an open and shut case. But Blake was well aware that the gang boss was more slippery than a wet fish. How else had he managed to evade capture for five years? And the longer the jury remained closeted in that small room behind the witness stand, the more Blake fretted. Marshal Cody Saggart tried to reassure the turncoat. But his half-hearted platitudes had little effect.

Blake tried persuading himself that his actions had been justified. For some time prior to the robbery he had been hankering to quit the gang. A life riding the owlhooter trail had its advantages. Plenty of dough in the good times, not to mention the dames. But there was always a down side. The constant worry of being nailed had done nothing for Blake's nervous system.

Few outlaws lasted more than a couple years before the law caught up with them – that or a bounty man's bullet. This was now Denny Blake's eighth year on the run, and the writing was most definitely on the wall. But quitting a guy like McCabe was easier said than done.

Nevada Tad Kettridge had made the break six months before. His body had been found riddled with bullets a week later down a stinking alleyway in Globe.

'Nobody quits the Arizona Raiders without my say so,' McCabe had declared pitching a caustic glare at the rest of the gang. 'Anyhow, ain't it bad manners to walk away without a word of thanks? There's gratitude for you.' He hawked out a mirthless guffaw before going on to outline the details of their next job. The others dutifully nodded their concurrence. It didn't do to challenge the boss when he was all stirred up.

No difficulty was experienced in finding a replacement. Argo Dunlop was a hard-nosed gunman known to McCabe from his days running with the Border Ruffians after the war. But from the very start, he and Blake had clashed. On more than one occasion McCabe had been forced to intervene when a show-down blew up. Dunlop was one more reason that prompted the outlaw to quit the gang. He prayed now to a God he had long ignored that his decision had been the right one.

Blake attempted a spirited return glower across the courtroom. But it lacked menace. He could feel the arrows of hate pinning his sweating carcase to the chair. Where in thunderation was that blamed jury? The murmuring of the crowd discussing the issue went over his head. Blake's head was filled with a maelstrom of churning thoughts as he once again played back over the events of the doomed raid. Had it only been a month before? To Denny the time had dragged by inexorably as he waited for the circuit judge to arrive in Spindriff.

The Raiders had made camp some five miles south of the town in a draw hidden from prying eyes. McCabe's intention was to hit the bank at closing time. As they waited to mount up, Blake plucked a yellow flower from a stand of columbine and pinned it to his vest. It was meant to be a highly visible announcement to the waiting townsmen of his non-involvement in the robbery. 'Yellow is my lucky colour,' the Judas outlaw responded trying to bury any hint of edginess when questioned by the wary gang leader. 'That's why I always wear a yellow shirt.'

'Goddamned nancy boy,' Dunlop muttered under his breath. Luckily for him the insult went unheard.

McCabe shrugged. It was of no consequence. Instead his attention focused on the forthcoming assault. 'There's reckoned to be twenty grand in banknotes sitting in that bank vault. And all just waiting for some enterprising dudes like us to pick up.' Shimmering peepers chock full of greed had already forgotten the incident of the columbine; a mistake that was to have dire consequences. 'Denny reckons it's to pay the miners for the gold they've dug out. But we're gonna divert the payoff into our pockets.' Gleeful bouts of chuckling broke out among the outlaws, with which Blake lustily joined.

Cantering at a steady pace the six desperadoes reached the edge of Spindriff some half an hour later, where McCabe signalled a halt. One final reminder was issued to men already tensed up in anticipation of the imminent lawless venture. 'Stay cool, boys. And keep your guns holstered until we get inside that bank.' His next bluff order was for the gang's wrangler. Bronco Vegas and his buddy, Sandpiper knew exactly what to do. But they dutifully nodded to appease the boss. 'Keep them nags facing outwards, ready and waiting for a quick getaway.'

The gang had ridden into Spindriff in pairs to avoid being noticed. All six arriving at once would immediately have raised suspicions. McCabe, Blake and the two others converged on the bank from opposite directions, casually leading their horses, which were tied up outside. The boss paused, casting a quick look around to ensure they had not attracted any unwelcome attention. Satisfied, he then pushed open the door.

Gun firmly pointing one way, he wasted no time. 'Okay, you lucky people, this is a stick-up,' he shouted out briskly. Eyes glittered with the thrill, the danger of the moment. Joe McCabe enjoyed nothing more than living on the edge. Pitting his perverted wits against the establishment was the outlaw's stock in trade. And bank robbery was his speciality. The cigar stuck in his mouth glowed red. 'Keep your hands high and you'll all leave here healthy if not happy.' A brittle laugh greeted his own quip, then it was down to business.

A quick flick of the head saw Chavez, Blake and Dunlop hustling towards the open bank vault. Each was carrying a flour sack. Neither of the tellers moved a muscle. They had all been advised about the forthcoming raid and ordered to display no resistance. Not that any was likely with the infamous bank robber snarling at them. 'Just take the notes,' McCabe rapped out. 'And make it snappy. We need to be out of here in three minutes flat.'

The raid went exactly as planned. No problems, a dream heist. Had he stopped to think, Joe might have reached the conclusion that it was a sight too darned easy. But all his thoughts were on lifting the dough and escaping back to the hidden draw from whence they had emerged.

Grabbing a hold of the heavy flour sack from Dunlop, McCabe checked the contents before backing out of the door on to the boardwalk. Denny Blake made sure to stay at the rear, ostensibly to keep a check on the tellers. He had no wish to be in the firing line when the shooting started. The men holding the horses quickly mounted up as the boss along with Chavez and Dunlop joined them.

That was when everything went haywire. A voice, gravelly and rasping with age yet urgently trenchant, called out from the shelter of a wagon on the far side of the street. 'Throw down your weapons and surrender peaceably. You turkeys are under arrest for armed robbery.' The lawman's orders to his newly sworn deputies were not to open fire unless the robbers displayed any resistance.

Stuck out in the open, surprise, disbelief even of suddenly being challenged momentarily stunned the men into immobility. Things had been going so well. What in tarnation had happened? Silence followed the ultimatum. Nary a sound from man nor beast could be heard as the heartbeat of time registered a glitch.

But Smokin' Joe had not become Arizona's most notorious gang boss by losing his head when confronted with a crisis. A rapid eye scan revealed the positions of half a dozen watchers. But he did not panic. Crisp orders were snapped out. 'Dig them spurs in, boys, and eat dust!'

The spell had been broken. All hell now erupted on the main street of Spindriff. Under Marshal Saggart's direction, the best shots with a rifle had been placed in strategic positions atop the roofs of surrounding buildings. Others covered both ends of the street to prevent a dash for freedom. The rest were secreted in adjacent buildings.

Vegas and Sandpiper were already mounted. Shooting blindly and without any further prompting they slapped leather and galloped off up the street. Their bodies were flattened low to present as small a target as possible. The ploy worked as bullets zipped by over their heads. But the two sharpshooters at the far end knew their business and easily plucked Sandpiper from his horse.

Vegas escaped injury, unlike his mount which was struck in the withers by two bullets. The animal stumbled and fell, its rider tossed into the air like a rag doll. But the instinct for survival is the most powerful of sentiments. Scrambling to his feet the wrangler sprinted for the cover of some barrels. He never made it as five bullets slammed into his back.

Cast afoot, McCabe desperately returned fire, diving behind a nearby water trough. His two henchmen were left floundering in the street. Standing side by side with guns drawn, they had little to aim at. Cock and fire, cock and fire. The end soon came as both men were riddled with hot lead. Only Smokin' Joe remained untouched. The trademark cigar was still gripped tightly between clenched teeth. But not for long if'n he remained where he was. McCabe was trapped like a rat in a barrel, and unless he acted quickly the end would be a hole on Boot Hill.

In the thick of the action with bullets flying every which way, he had given no thought to Denny Blake.

Only now, crouched behind the trough with bullets ricocheting off in all directions, did he assume the guy was making his own stand somewhere down the street. The fleeting inference was forgotten amid his own need to escape. It was now a question of survival of the fittest. Every man for himself.

And the chance presented itself immediately to his left where a narrow passage offered his one chance of escaping the lethal barrage. Death-dealing slugs ripped slivers of wood from the raised boardwalk as he slithered on all fours into the gloomy confines of the alley. Somehow he made it to safety without being hit. Alas, the spirited race to the far extremity saw his hopes dashed. The supposed escape route terminated in a dead end. A brick wall ten feet high blocked any chance of a getaway.

But the ruthless despot was not about to give in without a fight. He swung on his heels, six shooter panning the light at the street end.

'You ain't going nowhere, Joe.' The gruff diktat came from Cody Saggart. 'Except to Hell in a wooden overcoat if'n you've a mind.' The lawman was blocking any chance of escape. This was the end of the line. Back to the wall, the solitary figure at the end of the alley stood hunched down ready to meet Old Nick in person.

Then another voice echoed down the dirty passageway. One he knew only too well. The voice of the one gang member he had trusted above all others. 'Don't be a fool, Joe. There's ten guns aimed at your heart right now. You don't stand a chance.' Denny

Blake! The treacherous skunk had double-crossed him. The betrayal felt like he had been stabbed in the heart.

Smokin' Joe was so incensed he was almost tempted to go out in a blaze of gun smoke and glory. But that would play into the hands of that Judas. No, he would surrender and do his time.

A measured reply, self-assured and lacking rancour sounded all the more menacing in its delivery 'Okay, you win, Marshal, I'm coming out.' Slowly, at a leisurely pace, he walked back up the alley. His next words were for the Judas. 'You listen up good, Denny, cos one day I'll get out of the pen. And I'll hunt you down. There won't be a place you can hide that I won't suss out. Think on that while I'm gone. And may the Devil be sitting on your shoulder. It sure won't be Lady Luck.'

'Throw down your guns and keep them hands high.' This from Marshal Saggart who had been joined by the other townsmen.

MacCabe's attempt to intimidate his nemesis was brushed aside by the intended recipient. 'Don't make threats you can't keep, Joe.' Blake hawked out a scornful guffaw. 'You'll be a broken old man when Yuma lets you go. And I'll still be a spring chicken. No contest. Lock the bastard up, Marshal.'

All eyes being fastened on the captured desperado, they failed to heed the badly wounded Argo Dunlop who had managed to crawl beneath the boardwalk. He also was spitting feathers that the gang member he so despised had shopped them.

The innate fury lent him unknown strength to emerge from hiding. Blood was seeping from numerous bullet wounds as he lumbered to his feet, swaying like a newborn calf. All he could think of was finishing the rat off.

It was Marshal Saggart who perceived the alien presence to their rear. That sixth sense that every good lawman needs to survive now came into play. He swung round just in time to see the gun aimed at Blake's back. Two bullets triggered from the hip prevented a catastrophe. Dunlop staggered back, tumbling into the trough that had so recently protected his boss. The water quickly turned a dull red.

'Much obliged, Marshal,' Blake gasped out breathing deeply with relief. 'I owe you for that.'

'I didn't do it to save your hide, mister,' the ageing tinstar retorted. 'We need your testimony to book this varmint a long holiday in Yuma.' Quickly he turned back to ensure Smokin' Joe had not taken advantage of the brief skirmish to make a break. He need not have worried. There were enough townsmen to ensure the outlaw boss was well and truly neutralized.

Blake's cogitations were interrupted by the usher's command for all to stand as the jury returned to deliver its verdict. 'Have you reached a verdict upon which you are all agreed?' intoned the judge in a suitably sombre voice.

'We have, your honour,' came back the foreman's equally grave reply.

'Prisoner will stand and face the jury.' McCabe reluctantly struggled to his feet, the heavy shackles rattling in protest, before Judge Askew continued. 'So do you find the defendant guilty or not guilty?'

A pause to swell the tension. Lem Carney, the local bank manager and foreman, was not about to let this moment pass without every man in the courtroom hanging on his announcement. His name would be writ large in the papers. And when it came there was uproar. 'Guilty!'

The judge waited until the tumult had died down before announcing the sentence. 'You, Joseph McCabe, have been found guilty of a most heinous crime. We will not tolerate such lawless conduct in Arizona. You will go to prison for . . . twenty years. Take him away!'

Immediately three guys with press cards stuck in their hats rushed out. Each was intent on being the first to get this momentous news into print. They all mounted up and rode off hell for leather in different directions. Spindriff was a remote settlement forty miles from the nearest town of any size with a newspaper. And that happened to be the *Tucson Herald*. Within days, the news of McCabe's capture and imprisonment would be splashed across the territory and beyond.

Denny Blake couldn't stop a manic grin creasing up his face. But McCabe was not about to accept this verdict without a spiritedly intense rejoinder. 'Someday I'll get out of Yuma and I'll be back to burn this dump to the ground. The Devil on horseback will pour down his wrath on you bunch of hay-seeds and rename it Hellfire.' Still ranting all manner of vitriolic threats, Smokin' Joe was dragged away, but his pointing finger pinned Blake to his seat, sending a shiver down the turncoat's spine. 'And you, mister, will be sitting atop the funeral pyre.'

CHAPTER TWO

TWO YEARS LATER AND AN OFFER REFUSED

The nearer that Rick Norton came to the town of Spindriff, the more his thoughts harked back to an ignominious departure three years before. But more to the point, how would the good citizens who had ostracized him react to his unexpected return? It was unlikely to be a harmonious welcome. Indeed, he was more than likely to receive a frosty reception. Even hostile.

Those bastards had been all set to hang him from the nearest tree. It was only at the urging of Marshal Cody Saggart, claiming for him the time-honoured right of self defence, that he had escaped unscathed. The two had always been friends. But the lawman's hands were tied. He had to carry out the bidding of the town council. When the delegation finally accepted that a charge of murder could not be proven in a court of law, Saggart was forced to uphold the council's firm stipulation that Rick Norton should be banished.

Rick discarded the notion with a careless shrug. He had done nothing wrong. It was a handful of those bigoted council officials who had turned the town against him. Well they could go sup with the Devil. He had more important matters to take care of. Matters of an unsettling nature. Once again he removed the wire sent by his old pal. It had finally caught up with Rick in Prescott.

It read: *Your pa found dead in front of cabin. Heart attack suspected. Now lying in town cemetery.* That was all. But it was enough to find the itinerant gambler heading for home. If'n he could still call it that. With his father no longer alive, what had become of the old homestead? He picked up the pace to a steady canter.

Since being exiled from Spindriff on account of his prowess with a six-shooter, Rick had drifted around, never stopping in one place too long. He was a practised card wielder so had no trouble earning a good living. The boom towns of Arizona attracted a host of nefarious hucksters as well as naïve gold prospectors. Cheats on both sides of the divide were commonplace, and Rick had learned to handle them all with ruthless dexterity.

Such was his acquired reputation, young pretenders of all description now challenged him just for the sake of gaining that all-important status as the guy who outdrew Rick Norton. Graveyards across the territory were littered with the unlucky victims of his legendary trigger finger. It was a rep he could have well done without. But once gained, such a degree of notoriety was hard to cast off.

He fingered the red locket bearing pictures of both his parents. The cherished keepsake had been donated by his father after Martha Norton had succumbed to the fever. Rick wore it with pride around his neck. That was the principal reason he had adopted the red queen of hearts as his favourite card, the one now stuck in his hat band. It had also led to him being given the sobriquet of Red Spot. Anyone questioning the origin of the name or the card was given short shrift.

Unintentionally, owing to his mind being occupied by the mysterious wire, Rick's horse had wandered off the trail. It was an easy mistake to make amidst the bleak and unforgiving terrain of the Maricopa Sink. Salt bush dominated the arid landscape interspersed with clumps of tamarisk and catclaw. And nobody could ignore the towering saguaro cacti, some of which were around when the first Spanish Conquistadores invaded the new world.

So it came as a blunt shock when he was challenged by a gruff voice.

'Hold up there, stranger,' the hidden sentinel called out. 'One false move and you're buzzard bait.' Surprise at being suckered was splashed across the craggy face. But he did as bidden, raising his hands to prevent any adverse reaction from a nervous trigger finger. 'Just keep riding ahead while I follow,' the guy added, emerging from behind a boulder. 'The boss will be mighty interested to learn why some jasper is snooping around near our camp.'

'Can I put my hands down to control my horse?' Rick asked.

'Just keep 'em held high,' was the blunt order. 'Looks like the cayuse is doing just fine on her own.'

Ten minutes passed before the duo arrived at a shallow depression where upwards of a dozen men were sprawled around a fire shovelling grub down their throats. They all stiffened on seeing a stranger arriving in their hidden encampment. Hands dropped to gun butts. The array of weaponry visibly on display ensured that Rick kept his own mitts raised. One of them quickly relieved him of his six-gun.

A tough-looking *hombre*, his scowling face ravaged by pox scars, slowly stood up. Instantaneously Rick knew he would need all his wits to walk away from this rattlers' nest unscathed. The hulking bruiser was clearly the leader. His cold-eyed gaze lacked any hint of benevolence, mean and calculating with a ruthless streak. A critter who had clearly sold his soul to the devil. The jasper removed the stub of a cigar from between teeth stained yellow and casually brought it back to life with a sliver of burning wood. 'So what have we here, Concho?' he coughed, hawking out a lump of goo that sizzled in the fire.

'Caught this guy sneaking around at the mouth of

the arroyo, boss,' the man called Concho replied, signalling for his prisoner to dismount. 'I figured you'd
want to have words, or maybe something more permanent.'

'You thought right,' the gang leader snapped
back. 'So what's your game, mister? Mooching
around in this godforsaken wilderness ain't good for
the health.'

Effecting an outwardly laid-back mien far removed
from the tight knot in his guts, Rick met the rough
jasper's gaze head on. 'I could ask you the same question.' His eyes panned across the hovering gunmen.
'A platoon of jaspers all tooled up? Don't strike me
like you're going to a Sunday school picnic.'

The gang leader stiffened. A leery snarl bent his
stubble-coated features out of shape. Just as quickly
his manner relaxed, a roar of laughter emerging
from the open maw. He slapped his thigh. 'I like it,'
he announced to all and sundry. 'This fella has balls
addressing me like that.' The hardcase paused,
jabbing a thumb into his own chest. 'Clearly you
don't cotton to who you're dealing with here, mister.
Tell him, Stretch,' he ordered a lean-limbed stick
more akin to a thin trickle of pump water.

'This is Smokin' Joe McCabe, notorious leader of
the Arizona Raiders,' Stretch snapped out on cue.
'So I suggest you show him due respect if'n you want
to stay upright.'

The newcomer's raised eyebrows registered surprise, much to McCabe's delight, indicating that he
certainly had heard the name and its notoriety. 'Easy

there, Stretch, I like a fella that has spunk. Just so long as he knows who's in charge. Give the guy a drink,' he said signalling for another of his men to pour Rick a drink of coffee. A splash of whiskey was added to spice it up.

The strong brew was gratefully accepted. Rick nodded his appreciation. 'Sure I've heard of you. Who ain't in these parts. We've never met but I've heard some mighty fancy tales that would make Old Nick himself blush.'

'And all true,' McCabe chuckled uproariously. 'I can guarantee it.'

The interjection was ignored. 'I heard tell you were stuck in Yuma on a twenty stretch.'

A growl of disdain cut short the remark. 'The dump ain't been built that can hold a sharp dude like me. I did two years then managed to escape from a work detail three months ago. These fellas were more than happy to join me for where I'm headed. Ain't that so, boys?' Grunts of accord greeted the query. 'But you still haven't answered my question.'

The light-hearted banter of moments before had dissolved as a dozen pairs of eyes homed in on the interloper. Rick felt like a hunted rabbit as he sucked in a deep breath. 'I'm headed for Spindriff. I was dozing in the saddle and my horse must have drifted off the trail.'

McCabe's studied gaze narrowed, the black orbs probing from beneath hooded eyebrows. 'Spindriff, you say.' It was a statement rather than a question. 'Seems like we're headed the same way, fella. I'm wondering if that's a twist of fate or something more sinister.'

Both men sipped their coffee while Rick fashioned a suitable reply. 'I have business there. Personal business.'

That was when the penny dropped. McCabe's eyes widened on spotting the playing card stuck in Rick's hat band. 'Well, I'll be a lop-eared mule. You're Rick Norton.' Now it was McCabe's turn to display some regard. He stood up giving his guest a mock bow. 'We're highly honoured, boys. This guy has form. Let me present the slick gambler they call Red Spot. Not quite on a level with me, but he deserves our respect. So what's with the painted lady in your hat?'

'That's my concern and it ain't up for discussion.' The renowned gambler's rejoinder was brittle. He was not about to explain himself to this *desperado*.

McCabe thought for a moment before deciding not to pursue the matter. 'Suit yourself. I don't question a man's business . . . unless, of course, it affects me. I hear tell you also have a reputation for being a slick gunhand. Is that a bold fact, or just a load of hot air?'

'Better ask the jaspers who figured I talked too much.'

A crafty half smile creased the gang leader's face. 'Maybe we'll find out someday. But for the moment I have more important matters to discuss. Rumour has it you left Spindriff under a cloud. Upset the good citizens with some fancy gunplay.' Rick made no effort to dispute the assertion. 'So it seems to me that you ain't gotten no love for the place.' McCabe leaned across and added another shot to Rick's mug. 'There's a heap of dough sitting in yonder bank and I intend to take it, then burn that dump to the ground like I promised when those turkeys sent me to the pen. They're gonna get one helluva shock when I turn up early.'

'Why you telling me all this, Joe?' Rick enquired accepting a cigar from the voluble hardcase. 'I could be working for the Pinkertons.'

'If'n I thought that for a moment, you'd be a dead duck by now.' Joe thrust his bullet head forward. The warped smirk bending his leathery visage was meant to intimidate. Rick remained taciturn, unyielding. His life depended on displaying an equal degree of machismo. Any sign of weakness and this braggart would toss him to the wolves. It was McCabe who broke eye contact first. He threw the butt end of his cigar into the fire and lit up a fresh one.

'You and me are alike, Red Spot. We both have reason to hate that berg,' he declared feeling magnanimous. 'I could sure use a guy of your standing to help me out. Why don't we join up?' He leaned over and grabbed the whiskey bottle tipping a liberal slug down his throat. 'I'll make it worth your while. At the same time you can have your revenge on the town that's done the dirty on us both.' McCabe smiled, then sat back, certain that the famous gambler would fall in with his suggestion.

Rick took his time answering, all the while holding the gang leader's attention with a deadpan look.

'What I have to do in Spindriff, I'm doing alone.'

The smile evaporated from McCabe's face faster than a puddle under the desert sun. In its place a testy glare augured badly for the uninvited guest. 'So that's your game,' he snarled out, back rigid as a tent pole. 'Hoping to lift that dough all on your ownsome. Well, it ain't gonna happen.'

Rick's response was immediate. He was fully cognisant of how McCabe would react to his refusal to join the Raiders. Without any hesitation the hot coffee was tossed into McCabe's face. At the same time he kicked over the cooking gear and lunged at the floundering villain, grabbing him around the neck. The guy's own hogleg was quickly palmed and jammed into his ear. 'Any of you jaspers move a muscle and Joe will vanish in a puff of his own smoke. Now unbuckle those belts and toss 'em away.'

Nobody moved, leaving the order hanging in the air. Hostile eyes wavered, unable to absorb the sudden change in fortunes. Rick tightened his grip causing the captive outlaw some anguish. 'Tell 'em, Joe. You're history in three seconds unless those guns get shucked.'

McCabe was under no illusions that Red Spot Norton would carry out his threat. 'Do as he says, boys,' he gurgled. Bulging peepers flickered left to the shadow of death grinding into his head. 'This critter ain't joking.'

In moments the outlaws had complied allowing Rick to drag his reluctant hostage over to where his horse was tethered. Then he tentatively mounted up.

'Grab a hold of the horn. We'll walk aways together until I'm out of pistol range.' His next order was for the confused gang. 'Any of you guys decide to follow and the Smoker here breathes his last.' Slowly the rider and his subdued companion moved away from the campsite.

When he felt ready to make a dash for freedom, Rick boot-heeled the cursing brigand in the back sending the varmint sprawling headlong into a clump of cholla cactus. McCabe hollered painfully as the sharp thorns dug into his exposed flesh, enabling Rick to make good his getaway.

But the angst-ridden wailing soon brought his cohorts scurrying along to help their boss. The men gathered round offering their assistance in his hour of need. Laughter at the frantic efforts of McCabe to dislodge the needle points from his anatomy might have occurred to the brigands. But every face remained suitably blank at the abuse dished out to the vanished source of his predicament.

A lion is always at its most dangerous when injured. McCabe ranted and raved at what he would do to the skunk next time they met up. And that would be soon if immediate action was taken. 'Clancy and Jumbo,' he called out to his two best trackers. 'Grab your horses and go after that no-good. Take him alive, then bring the critter back here. He can't get far in this country. Now shift your asses!'

The pursuers were soon heading off in the direction taken by their recent visitor. Unlike that of their quarry, the outlaw mounts were well rested and quickly able to pick up the clear trail left by the fugitive. Urged on by prodding spurs, the horses flew like the wind, twisting and turning between the rocky spurs and clumps of saltbush littering the wild terrain. Coyotes and foxes scuttled out of the way to avoid pounding hoofs as the chasers ploughed onward.

It was Clancy who first spotted the tell-tale signs that they were overhauling the fugitive. A yip of triumph emerged from the pursuer's open maw while pointing to the rising tendrils of dust up ahead. 'Won't be long now, pal. That nag of his'n will be tiring fast.' The two men exchanged lurid grins while grasping their hoglegs.

Even though he had not heard the verbal comment from his pursuer, Rick sensed they were gaining on him. His horse was indeed tiring fast, its pace slackening markedly. The animal's flanks were coated in a white sheen of lather, its nostrils flaring. His first intimation that the pursuit was nearing its climax was heralded by a volley of bullets zipping past his head.

All too soon the inevitable happened. The horse faltered. Stumbling, it almost unseated its rider. Rick threw a glance behind and saw blood spurting from a direct hit to the mare's rump. Before he had a chance to think, the animal pitched forwards, flinging its rider head over heels on to the hard ground. Rick knew that his life depended on swift reflexes. The blurry effects of the tumble were shrugged off as he scrambled to his feet.

The two riders hammered around a bend into view, catching Rick in the open. Legs splayed akimbo for balance, he stood his ground, pumping a full chamber of bullets at them. His final round struck paydirt. Clancy yelled out and bit the dust. His pudding-shaped buddy veered off behind some rocks. But with his victim cast afoot and gun now empty, Jumbo knew he had the upper hand. 'Won't be long now, Red Spot,' the outlaw called out in manic jubilation. 'And I'm gonna make certain your end is slow and painful for gunning down my best pal.'

The outlaw's chilling ultimatum sent a shiver of dread racing down his intended victim's spine. Rick dashed towards a nearby cluster of boulders piled high like slabs of sourdough bread. Scrambling up a narrow gully he just managed to round the bend at its head when Jumbo appeared below. Bullets chewed lumps of rock inches from his head.

The clatter of hoofs echoed up the gully as the pursuer gave chase. But a horse in such confined terrain was a hindrance, affording Rick the opportunity to disappear amidst the boulder-strewn wasteland. From there he was able to clamber up on to a ledge, pausing to reload the revolver taken from Smokin' Joe. Luckily the guy had good taste in hand guns, and the popular .45 Colt Frontier took the same ammo as his own Peacemaker with the shorter barrel.

Moments later the rattle of stones found Rick crawling towards the edge of the shelf. The jungle hunter's eyes shifted around trying to locate his quarry. But they failed to lift skywards. A potentially fatal error of judgement. Hunkered down on all fours, Rick waited like a hungry puma, readying himself to pounce when the guy passed beneath his perch.

He flew through the air dragging Jumbo off his horse. The jasper didn't know what had struck him. His unwieldy bulk proved a distinct encumbrance to any swift retaliation. Rick gave him no time to recover. A couple of hard jabs were quickly delivered to the chin effectively terminating the pursuit in the potential victim's favour. The winner of the uneven contest used the outlaw's own lariat to truss him up tighter than a Thanksgiving turkey. And looking like a fell-fed specimen to boot, which gave Rick cause for some rare hilarity.

Satisfied that Jumbo posed no further threat, he then none too gently slapped the rotund kisser to bring him round. 'Wake up, Jumbo. They say that an elephant never forgets. Guess you won't forget this in a hurry.' The witty aside caused further laughter at Jumbo's expense.

'W-what happened?' the groggy outlaw burbled.

'I reckon you need some extra lessons in success-ful tracking,' Rick declared breezily before assuming a more sombre tone. 'Now listen up good. I have a message for that two-bit villain you call a boss. Tell McCabe from me that nobody messes with Red Spot Rick Norton.' He paused, grabbing the guy by his shirt front and shaking him like a bag of flour. 'You

31

listening, fat boy? He'd do well to give Spindriff a wide berth. There ain't gonna be nothing for him there but grief and hot lead.'

He then bundled the outlaw on to his horse. 'Ain't you gonna release me?' Jumbo complained, holding up his tethered hands. Although in truth, he was more than glad to be still breathing.

'You'll manage,' was the blunt reply as Rick slapped the horse on its rump. 'And if'n you can't, the nag sure can.'

CHAPTER THREE

A GRAVE DECLARATION

Rick made good his escape by commandeering Clancy's horse. The dazed Jumbo was left to make his way back to the outlaw camp. He knew that the advice delivered to McCabe would be ignored. The gangster chief had lost face and would need to reassert his authority. Any sliver of human feeling buried in that brutish torso would have been smothered. The good citizens of Spindriff were most definitely in for a rough time.

Not that Rick cared a hoot about their feelings. Many of them, especially those pompous councillors, had wanted to string him up to the nearest tree following that incident with Brad Quindle and his sons. He had Cody Saggart to thank for his life. But Spindriff was still his town, the place where he had been raised. And he considered himself duty bound to issue a stark warning of McCabe's intentions.

Not everyone was like Harvey Rizzlock and Lem Carney. Some good people lived there who didn't deserve the treatment likely to be meted out by the Arizona Raiders. They had to be warned and urged to prepare for battle. One in which blood would more than likely be spilled.

Being familiar with the area, Rick was aware that he needed to reach Spindriff quickly. A direct ride as the crow flies was possible by taking the old miners' trail south through the abandoned ghost town of Contention and over the Eagletail Mountains by way of Sentinel Pass. The tough part would be crossing the waterless expanse of the Sand Tank. Nothing but desiccated mesquite, sagebrush and the ubiquitous saguaro. It should take no more than three days if'n he pushed the hijacked roan hard enough.

He was making a big assumption that this was alien territory to McCabe, who accordingly he expected to follow the regular route and so avoid getting lost. That should give the town enough time to prepare a suitably hot reception for the bandit gang. But he would need to keep on the move. Chewing on sticks of beef jerky helped to keep up his strength.

There was one water hole on this side of Sand Tank at Baxter Springs where the short cut rejoined the regular trail. A lone cross marked the grave of its discoverer. The bleached bones of Prospector Ed Baxter were found years later no more than two yards beyond the thin trickle which he must have missed in the dark. It had since become a lifesaver for those traversing the infamous strip of desert. Dozing in the saddle, Rick pointed the roan in the right direction allowing the animal to pick its own course across the Sand Tank. The crossing was successfully achieved with a day to spare.

Soon after, Red Spot found himself on the edge of the town from which he had been ostracized three years before almost to the day. The familiar edifice of Porcupine Quill reached skyward on his right side. Mixed feelings raged through his body as he gazed down on the sleepy enclave. Anger at the unfair treatment meted out by arrogant bureaucrats jostled for supremacy with more personal sentiments concerning the fate of his father.

The town was named after another eccentric gold prospector with the poetic handle of Ebenezer Spindriff. Better known as Moonbeam, it was said he had lost his marbles searching for the legendary Lost Dutchman Mine* in the Superstition Mountains to the north-west.

Moonbeam did, however, come across a well here-abouts, and this became the main source of water around which the settlement of Spindriff developed. The crazy coot was shot dead by those who objected to paying good money when he tried to charge them five dollars for a canteen of the life-giving elixir. His nickname had also survived in the form of a large

*For more about the Lost Dutchman read Dale Graham's *Bad Deal in Buckskin*, a Black Horse Western also published by The Crowood Press.

white disc advertising Spindriff's premier house of entertainment, the Moonbeam Dancehall and Theatre.

'Now I wonder what sort of reception we're gonna find down there,' Rick mused aloud tweaking the roan's pointed ears. The mare snickered in reply. 'Guess you're right, old gal. Only way to find out is take the bull by the horns and venture into the lion's den. If'n that makes any darned sense.'

He nudged the horse down the slope passing a newly built extension to the schoolhouse on the edge of town. And on the far side, a gleaming white spire proclaimed the construction of a church. 'During my time, preaching the Lord's Word was carried on in the theatre,' he muttered under his breath, reaching the conclusion that Spindriff had clearly prospered during his enforced absence.

Recent settlers who obviously had no recollection of the infamous gambling gunslinger ignored the newcomer. But enough heads were turned by those who did recognize the rugged persona. Shock and more than a hint of trepidation showed on too many faces, perceiving that Spindriff's days of peace and quiet could be under threat. A mirthless half smile greeted the stark looks. If only they knew the truth.

By the time he reached the far side of the town and had dismounted outside the cemetery, word of his arrival had already reached official ears. A palpable tension fastened its insidious grip on the settlement as people whispered to each other about what it would mean for them. The nail-biting atmosphere went over Rick's head as he pushed through the iron gate and made his way over to his mother's grave. And there alongside was a second wooden epitaph where his father now lay.

A single teardrop traced a path through the dark stubble of his left cheek. Head bowed, he removed his hat clutching it tightly across his chest. Both parents now gone. His mother taken by a bout of fever. Now Pa, allegedly from a heart attack. His brow creased in thought. The old-timer had been as fit as a fiddle when he left. And the most recent letter he had picked up in Window Rock had given no indication of any ailments. The brief wire received from Cody Saggart had been signed with his new title *Retired Town Marshal.* His old pal must have passed responsibility for law and order to some other tin star.

Rick's eyes then shifted to the right. A cynical glower took in the rough sign hammered into the ground at the head of an open grave. It read: *Reserved for Rick Norton.* There was even a spade stuck in the pile of dirt ready to fill the grave with its assigned corpse, namely himself.

'Baz Quindle has sworn to shoot you on sight and fill in that grave himself for gunning down his kin and chasing off young Billy.' The grim avowal saw Rick spinning round. A man of around his own age boasting a fine black moustache waxed at the ends stood facing him. He was holding a gun aimed at Rick's heart. But it was the badge glinting in the sunlight that caught his eye. 'Denny Blake, town marshal,' the guy introduced himself.

Rick acknowledged the double-edged welcome with a curt nod of the head. 'No need for the gun, marshal. I don't want no trouble.'

'Glad to hear it. But your reputation makes me a mite nervous,' the lawman espoused, keeping the Smith & Wesson Schofield steady. 'Quindle claims the charge of murder ought to have seen you dangling from a rope's end. Reckons it was only due to the previous incumbent sowing doubt in the heads of enough council members that saved your neck.' He nodded towards the two graves further back.

A growl of derision gurgled in Rick's throat on reading two identical epitaphs. 'Those skunks weren't murdered. It was them who wanted me dead. Brad Quindle claimed that I cheated him at cards.' Rick scoffed at the notion. 'Poor losers always allege the dealer is at fault. I've always run a straight game.' He tapped the red queen in his hat. 'My ma would be turning in her grave if'n she figured her son was nought but a two-bit tinhorn. Those critters would have ambushed me if'n I hadn't learned about their lowdown plot. And that darned council knew it.'

'That's as maybe. You don't need to convince me, fella. It was before my time,' Blake declared, not yet ready to place any trust in the infamous prodigal. 'But they employ me to keep the peace. Nobody seems to want you hanging around.' A macabre smile creased the lawman's face. 'Sorry about the wisecrack. It just kind of slipped out.' Rick's thin slash of a mouth paled as he returned the smile. 'They're tired of too many drifters coming here hoping to challenge the famous Red Spot.'

'My heart bleeds for them.'

The cynical remark passed over Blake's head. He had been told to get rid of this irritant. And having been given the job, he intended to do just that. Nevertheless, the lawman couldn't help but harbour some degree of respect for the guy. Sympathy even. 'I can understand why you came back to pay your respects. But you've done that, so I suggest you get moving and don't stop until you reach the border.'

'Maybe the good folks of Spindriff won't be so eager to see the back of a handy gunslinger like me when they hear what else I'm here for.' The sarcastic overtone was not lost on the outlaw-turned-lawman.

Blake stroked his chin, offering the doughty stranger a thoughtful nod. 'So how's about enlightening me,' he suggested, 'if'n it's so danged important.'

'There's a gang of bad hats heading this way. They aim to rob the bank and burn this place to the ground.' The startling announcement certainly caught Blake's attention. 'And they'll be here in two days, so you'll need to get these critters organized if'n you intend saving this town from going up in smoke.'

Seconds stretched into minutes while Blake struggled to absorb this disquieting piece of news. He could barely take it in. Eventually his face twisted, displaying a frown cloaked in scepticism. The luxuriant moustache twitched as he attempted to work out the veracity of the contention. 'How do I know this ain't just some vengeful ploy to frighten the folks you figure have done the dirty on you?'

'I happened upon their camp north of here in the Maricopa Sink. The leader was mighty peeved with this town. A sight more so than me, if truth be told.'

'Go on,' Blake pressed, now all ears. 'Let's have it. What's his beef?'

'He wants revenge on the critters that sent him to Yuma,' Rick watched as the blood drained from the other man's face. The ghastly truth was slowly dawning, confirmed by the gunslinger's next assertion. 'And on one guy in particular who shopped him to the law.' Rick didn't need to elaborate. 'That's right, fella. Smokin' Joe is out, escaped from a chain gang. And the critter is hell bent on retribution.'

Blake's legs almost gave way. The gun slipped from his fingers. Slumping down on a gravestone, an ice-cold shiver rippled through his sagging frame. A twenty-year spell in the pen for his erstwhile associate was now a mere flight of fancy. A bandanna dabbed nervously at the sweat coating his grey features. For a brief moment the turncoat's brain froze, unable to comprehend the magnitude of what he had just learned. And more to the point, what was soon to be unleashed. Finally he managed to blurt out, 'How many men does he have?'

'I counted twelve, but that was reduced by one when I fled the camp. So he's down to eleven. But they're all hardened gun toters.'

'I'd reckoned on being rid of that life,' Blake

40

muttered, half to himself. 'But I guess that was only a pipedream as well. Once you take the owlhooter trail, there ain't no turning back.' His fearful gaze swung as he addressed Rick. 'Guess you'll know all about that.'

Rick nodded his understanding. After witnessing the disdainful looks cast his way on first entering the town, his attitude had altered. Folks he had known all his life peering down their beaky snouts at him. That was enough to encourage him to sort out his personal business, then light out never to return. Why bother lending these miserable critters a hand? They can handle McCabe on their ownsome, if'n they're able. It was no concern of his.

The two unlikely collaborators mulled over their options and how best to move forward. The mind-boggling announcement of McCabe's return had certainly given the reformed outlaw something to think about. He stared ashen-faced into the distance. How should he handle it?

Rick studied the lawman's reaction, his thoughts following a similar direction. Some fellas would up sticks and skedaddle, head for the hills disappearing into the wide blue yonder. Was Denny Blake one of those? Best to give him the benefit of the doubt, for now at least. Here was a jasper who had broken away trying his darndest to go straight. That took guts. Rick was beginning to have second thoughts. Maybe he should stick around and offer his help.

And there were others who didn't deserve to be

left at the mercy of a blood-thirsty varmint like Smokin' Joe McCabe. Turning his back on trouble wasn't Rick Norton's way. It just didn't sit right. So the decision was made. 'I'm willing to back your play if'n you want,' he offered. 'Every man deserves the chance to make a fresh start. You appear to be doing just that.' He held out a hand.

The magnanimous gesture took Blake by surprise. He looked at the proffered appendage as if were a two-headed dog before accepting it. 'Much obliged, Rick.' Once the decision to face his demons and conquer them had been taken, Denny Blake shook off the lethargic torpor that had threatened to overwhelm him. He straightened up, shoulders squared, an injection of steel infusing his backbone. 'But I'll need to get those weak-kneed councillors to agree. Making a convincing argument that they need Red Spot Rick Norton's help ain't going to be easy.'

'I know you'll give it your best shot,' Rick averred. Nonetheless, he couldn't help feeling a sense of *déjà vu*. 'Let me know how they take it.' He hawked out a brittle laugh. 'Fellas like Harvey Rizzlock and Lem Carney are gonna choke on that humble pie they'll be forced to eat. But even they must know the consequences of going it alone.'

The two men split up. Rick's first call was to the general store run by Mayor Rizzlock. He needed some fresh supplies. Word of his arrival had clearly got around. More folks stopped in the street to eye the notorious gunfighter. Wives steered their husbands aside; likewise mothers with curious young sons, fearing that a fast gun hand went hand in glove with a quick temper. Rick was well used to such attention when visiting a new town. It was, nevertheless, somewhat unsettling in the place where he had grown up.

As he mounted the boardwalk in front of the store, a matronly dowager was loudly berating the mayor for allowing Rick Norton to walk the streets of Spindriff. 'That man should have been locked up the minute he arrived,' she spouted, receiving the stern support of her two equally starchy associates. 'Next thing we know he'll be shooting up the place. This is a quiet town and we want it to stay that way.' The snooty nose lifted with a supercilious sniff.

'I couldn't agree more,' the portly official concurred, receiving a spirited concurrence from his best friend Lem Carney. 'But until he steps out of line, I can't order the marshal to arrest him.'

'So someone has to be killed before you take any action? None of us are safe in our beds with that braggart roaming the streets.

'Disgraceful, I call it.' More sniffing and stamping of feet followed.

'Rest assured, ladies . . .' But that was as far as the toothless pledge went, as Rizzlock clapped eyes on the man in question who was leaning on the door post smirking. 'I g-guess . . .' he burbled, '. . . well, what I mean to say is. . . .'

Rick immediately helped the squirming official out. 'What the mayor is trying hard to say, Mrs Huckarby, is that he'd love to oblige, but not until he's served me.' Rick tipped his hat to the three ladies who quickly hustled away, abject terror written across their quivering faces. 'And a good day to you, too. Don't forget to tell everybody that Rick Norton will only be leaving Spindriff when he's good and ready.'

'So how's about you filling out this order I've prepared, Mister Mayor?' Rick said, briskly slapping the note on the counter. 'And don't worry, I ain't asking for credit. Good old US dollars earned fair and square will pay for these goods.' A cold regard challenged the storekeeper to suggest the dough was tainted.

Rizzlock's blotchy features assumed a ruddier colour than normal, his feet shifting about. Playing for time, he finished stacking some rakes in a corner while trying to figure out a suitable reply.

'I'm sorry, Rick. I'd like to help you. But I can't be seen doing business with a . . .' He gulped, unable to mouth the dreaded appendage: '. . . well, with a man like you. As Mayor of Spindriff, I have a certain responsibility to uphold. Folks won't take kindly to me abusing that position. You saw how old Ma Huckarby reacted. And she's president of the Women's Temperance League.'

Lem Carney butted in, trying to poor oil on troubled waters. 'Mexican Pete will help you out. He runs a store for the greaser population down Buckeye Street.' Straightaway he knew he had said the wrong thing.

Tight-lipped and gritting his teeth, Rick managed

to contain his anger. Did he really want to help pompous assholes like these turkeys out of a fix? 'Well, at least I know where I stand with the respectable citizens of this town,' he posited in a restrained tone of voice. 'Thanks a lot for being so understanding, gents.' And with that scratchy retort, he swung on his heel and left the store. 'I guess votes are more important than lives in your book.'

'What we gonna do about that fella, Harvey?' Carney asked his friend once Rick was out of earshot. 'We can't have him wandering the streets with Baz Quindle in town. There's bound to be trouble.'

'Don't you think I know that,' Rizzlock snapped, irritated by his associate's declaration of the obvious. 'If'n he sticks around, we'll have every gun-happy no-account in the territory heading for Spindriff. I'll have Blake give the critter his marching orders. Best thing is to make him realize there's no welcome for a gambling gunslinger in this town.'

Carney's bony head nodded in agreement. 'We have enough on our plate keeping all those gold prospectors in check.' He scratched his thinning pate of sandy hair. 'Come to think on it, I ain't seen many around for a few days.'

'A new strike has been discovered west of here up in the Turtle Creek country,' Rizzlock replied. 'Most everybody who can wield a pick and shovel has upped sticks and headed that way.'

An avaricious gleam appeared in Carney's eyes as he rubbed his claw-like hands together. 'And we both know where they'll be spending any paydirt they manage to dig out.'

For the moment, their unwelcome visitor was forgotten.

Rick meanwhile was heading down the street to call on the one person he knew would give him a warmer reception than he had received so far. The current lawman had told him that retired Marshal Cody Saggart was living in a cabin on the edge of town. Fists were bunched in anger as he neared the house. The dark cloud hanging over him would require more that his old buddy's good humour to disperse.

Irate thoughts fizzed and bubbled inside Rick's head. He needed more details about his pa's demise. And then there was Elly Jordan. How would she react to his return? They had been a serious item before all that trouble with the Quindles. A dog ran out of an alleyway yapping at his heels. But such was the prodigal's distraction that he paid it no heed. Even two young kids playing with wooden pistols, one claiming to be the infamous Red Spot Norton, failed to produce a reaction.

On he walked, oblivious to everything as his mind rehashed the grim events of that fateful day.

CHAPTER FOUR

PAST RECALL

Brad Quindle had come to town already half cut before he joined the game that Saturday night. There was no love lost between the two antagonists. Rick's father had bought some land that Quindle wanted in order to expand his own spread. The old guy's refusal to budge had irked the rancher. The Bar BQ rancher was unused to being denied what he sought.

He stumped into the Blue Parrot saloon accompanied by Ben and Billy, his two younger sons. All three must have been drinking heavily before they hit town, staggering into the Blue Parrot where Rick was employed as the house card-wielder. Their presence was announced in a loudly brash manner. Straightaway the house gambler knew that trouble was brewing. So when the strutting peacock lurched over to his table, Rick ignored Quindle's demand to join the game.

'You refusing to let me in?' slurred the inebriated rancher. 'Guess the tinhorn's scared that I'll clean up,' he blurted out to all those within earshot. Rick was loathe to admit drunks into any of his games. But Quindle was a member of the town council and could have his gambling license revoked. So, much to his later regret, he relented.

Quindle slumped down into a seat. 'So what you a-waiting on, tinhorn, Christmas?' The cold guffaw accompanying the noisy bluster had attracted a host of onlookers, all eager to watch the fun. 'Deal the cards.'

The game progressed for an hour, by which time the two other participants had folded, leaving only Rick and Brad Quindle to finish off. The rancher had been drinking steadily, and losing in a similar fashion. His warped features showed a man seething with indignation. He hated losing, especially to this peacock whose father had so recently humiliated him. The crucial hand saw a sizeable pot amassed in the centre of the green baize table. It had come down to the final call.

All eyes were on Quindle whose smirking pose hinted at a winning hand as he slowly laid down his cards. He lit up a cigar and deliberately puffed a cloud of smoke in his opponent's face. 'Beat that, Mister Red Spot.' Avarice oozed from every pore as the loud-mouthed cattleman reached out to claim the prize.

A firm hand from his opponent stayed the rake-in.

'I think you'll find that a straight tops three aces. The house wins.' Now it was Rick's turn to draw in the dough. Gasps went up from the startled onlookers. But it was towards the sore loser and his reaction to this bad defeat that all eyes now swung.

Rick fastened a meaningful eye on to the incensed loser. 'A good poker player always knows when to quit.' The thinly veiled insinuation implied that Brad Quindle was anything but. And the scornful leer accompanying that final imprudent remark was to prove Rick Norton's undoing. Jubilation at having defeated this strutting boaster overshadowed his innate caution.

Quindle's face turned a deep purple. 'You cheating bastard,' he growled out. 'That last hand was dealt from the bottom of the pack. You all saw it, didn't you boys?' Some of the more obsequious watchers in the crowd quickly agreed, spurred on by vociferous backing from Quindle's two sons. Most, however, remained silent.

But those few supporters were enough. Quindle lurched to his feet and made to draw his pistol. It was a clumsy and inept manoeuvre, easily surpassed by a man of Rick Norton's reputation. The gambler's gun hand, steady as a rock with the Colt revolver it contained, was sufficient inducement for the blusterer to recognize he was outclassed in that department. 'Don't try it, Brad. You lost fair and square. Why not come clean. Then we can shake on it and put this mistake behind us.'

But Quindle was having none of that. He jabbed

an accusatory finger at the man who had shamed him in front of everyone. 'I know you cheated me, Norton. And I ain't about to let this lie,' the Bar BQ boss snarled, jabbing a finger at the gambler. 'Don't be thinking you've heard the last of this. Nobody does the dirty on a Quindle.' With that threat hanging over the gathering, he stamped out of the saloon.

Rick quickly shook off the angry bluster spat out by the aggrieved rancher like raindrops from a wet slicker. It was merely drink talk. But Brad Quindle was an important man in Pima County. The Bar BQ was the biggest cattle spread around. As such he commanded substantial influence. Men took heed of his actions. And murmurings within the Blue Parrot should have given the hint that not everybody present concurred with the gambler's opinion. Rick was left alone, unaware that sceptical looks were mulling over the recent ugly scene.

Three days passed with no indication that the recalcitrant owner of the Bar BQ had any intention of fulfilling his drink-induced threat. Rick pushed the ugly incident to the back of his mind. In consequence he harboured no suspicion when a grubby urchin delivered a message that his father had fallen off his horse in Dead Horse Canyon. The old man had broken a leg and his cayuse had scarpered. He needed help badly.

Questions put to the boy elicited the assertion that the kid was returning from a fishing trip when he came across the injured man. 'He said for you to get out there pronto,' the boy ardently declared extending an optimistic hand. Rick flipped a dime into the air which the boy caught with a deft precision. A clear sign that he had done this sort of thing before. Rick's sly smirk soon dissolved. The disturbing essence of the news required his immediate attention.

Had he questioned the boy's story more carefully, he might well have uncovered disparities as to its veracity. For instance, the Dead Horse was a box canyon. What could his pa have been doing there? And it was drier than a Temperance Hall? No fishing within a day's ride. But that was with the benefit of hindsight. All Rick could think of was his father lying injured under a baking sun, unable to move.

In the blink of an eye, he was saddled up and heading south out of Spindriff. It was a two-hour ride to Dead Horse Canyon so there was no time to lose. Coincidence, luck, good fortune, call it what you will, was on Rick Norton's side that day. For who should come trotting towards him but the girl he was hoping to marry. Elly Jordan was a strikingly natural blonde and the prettiest gal in Pima County.

The pair had been walking out for some time. The girl had previously been courted by Baz Quindle. It was the guy's crude behaviour and distinct lack of decorum towards the opposite sex that had effectively terminated their relationship. Quindle felt shown up when the girl had turned her affections towards a mere tinhorn, and had threatened to get even.

Elly Jordan knew what she wanted from a man. And few could measure up to her high standards. Even Rick Norton. As a result, she had recently begun questioning the gambler's choice of career, not to mention his growing reputation for terminal gunplay, albeit of a defensive nature only. When Rick had suggested they get married and head for California, she had prevaricated, claiming it was a lot to ask and she needed time to consider such a drastic change of circumstance. Ever hopeful of a positive response, Rick had failed to heed the growing signs of disharmony.

So he greeted her now with his usual bonhomie. When she asked where he was heading, Rick poured out the news of his father's accident. Elly's adorable nose puckered, her brow crinkling in a frown of uncertainty.

'But that can't be true,' she disputed. 'I saw your pa only an hour since when I passed the holding. He was feeding the chickens. We exchanged greetings as I passed. He seemed perfectly all right to me.' A silence followed as both of them mulled over the implications of this startling development. 'Maybe the boy mistook you for somebody else,' Elly suggested.

Rick shook his head. 'He asked specifically for me in the Blue Parrot.' His brow furrowed as the grim truth began to dawn. This had to be a devious ruse thought up by the Quindles. 'It must have been sent by Brad Quindle. The sore loser accused me of cheating and threatened to have his revenge.' Rick was becoming good and mad. 'Him and those sons of his have lured me out to that remote canyon intending to lay an ambush. Well, they're gonna get the surprise of their miserable lives.'

Elly quickly butted in, grabbing a hold of his arm. An impulsive resort to gunplay that was consuming her beau had once again reared its ugly head. 'Let the marshal handle this, Rick,' she anxiously beseeched the angry man. 'You could easily get yourself killed. And there's plenty of others on that council who would like nothing more than to see Rick Norton thrown in jail. Turning vigilante will only play into their hands.'

But the girl's earnest plea had no effect. 'I ain't having skunks like the Quindles accusing me of cheating, then laying an ambush when I stand up to their bullying tactics.' Rick's obdurate stance was adamant. The stony regard told her in no uncertain terms that he would not be swayed from his lethal endeavour.

'Then be it on your own head.' She tossed her flowing tresses in annoyance at being rebuffed. Rick's immovably stubborn attitude was the straw that broke the camel's back. 'If that's your choice, then mine is that we're through. Anything that was between us is over. I want nothing more to do with a man headed for a certain burial with his boots on.' Tears dribbled down her cheeks.

Rick almost yielded to his sweetheart's anguish. But it was momentary. No guy worth his salt could allow himself to be walked all over. A man had his pride, his standing in the community to uphold, be it a respectable front like Rizzlock and Carney, or in Rick's case, a solid reputation as a man not to be crossed.

'Go home, Elly,' he said quietly trying to ease away the strain warping the girl's distraught features. 'Think it over. You'll see that my way is the only trail to follow. The West is a tough place and only those willing to stand up for their rights can survive out here.' And with that final remark, he nudged his horse forwards towards a destiny reliant on a man's ability to outwit his opponents with guile and a steady gun hand.

Elly watched him ride away. Had she been right to break off their relationship? Her father would certainly have no regrets on that score. As a deacon on the parish council of their local chapel, he had always vigorously expressed reservations about his only daughter consorting with a gambler, especially one carrying a reputation where gunplay was an ever distinct possibility.

But Elly Jordan was equally strong-willed in her own way. And parental disapproval for her choice of paramour was like a red rag to a bull. Only now did she come to the realization that no future was possible with a man like Rick Norton. However much her heart still fluttered on recalling his touch, in these uncertain times a girl needed security.

And local businessman Judd Farlow had been showing her undue attention of late. He had prospects that a girl would be foolish to ignore. Yes, she mused, the right course of action had been taken. Nevertheless, she had no wish to see any harm come to her former consort. And the Quindles were a ruthless bunch of hardcases who would resort to any sort of trickery to avenge an alleged affront. Accordingly she spurred off in the direction of Spindriff to seek help from Marshal Saggart.

Meanwhile, Rick had every intention of thwarting those bushwhacking varmints. And thanks to his meeting up with Elly, he was now fully cognizant of their heinous goal. He pushed her cold-shouldering of him aside, confident of being able to bring her round over a candle-lit dinner at the Prairie Oyster Eating House when this ugly business had been concluded.

His mind was now fully focused on foiling any skulduggery being hatched by Brad Quindle. And the intended victim knew that he held a winning hand. Prior knowledge of the ambush would enable him to catch the critters by surprise. Accordingly, he avoided the entrance to the canyon, picking out a tortuous route up through the amalgam of rocky outcrops on to the plateau above.

There he dismounted, leading the horse along the rim of the mesa. Eagle eyes scanned the enclosed rift of the canyon below, searching for any alien movement. Ten minutes later he spotted three horses tethered behind some boulders. Their riders had to be close by. He wasn't long in spotting his human prey. They were skulking behind a cluster of rocks completely oblivious of being under close scrutiny.

The bulky figure of Brad Quindle was flanked by two of his sons. Each of them was clutching a six-gun with all their attention directed towards the canyon entrance. Only Baz was absent. There was no sign of the elder sibling. He must be away someplace else. Rick's smile was cold as ice, frozen in a rictus that spoke of dire consequences in the offing. Any time for reconsideration was long past.

Slowly he picked his way down through the stony wilderness ensuring no sound was made to alert the bushwhackers. A startled prairie dog quickly disappeared down its burrow. A circling buzzard was observing the intruders from on high. It cawed once before continuing its search for more enticing prey. Closer and closer the hidden stalker crept.

He was about to call out for the skunks to surrender, when calamity struck in the form of a disturbed rattlesnake. So intent had Rick been on keeping his quarry in sight that he failed to heed the writhing beast. It was the sudden and deadly clicking of the tail bones that alerted him to the imminent danger. His reaction was automatic. Two shots blasted the striking threat out of existence. But the element of surprise had been lost.

Nevertheless, the three bushwhackers were equally confounded by this unexpected frustration of their odious scheme. They swung round to face the unforeseen attack. But Rick was first to recover his wits. His gun spoke twice more, dropping Ben Quindle who had made the fatal mistake of jumping to his feet. Panic gripped the remaining duo, both of

56

whom began recklessly triggering their revolvers without thought for accuracy.

With their kinsman sprawled in the sand, blood leaking from a punctured lung, any notion of caution on their part was stifled. Bullets flew every which way apart from into their intended target. These were cattle men, not gunslingers. In stark contrast, Rick held his nerve like any good gambler. A gritty resilience saw him facing his opponents square on. Here was a seasoned practitioner in the art of gunplay, fixedly stoic and determined under fire. His ballistic reply proved the point as the last two shells removed Brad from the unequal contest.

That was the moment young Billy's courage failed him completely. He threw down his gun, hands clawing at the sky. 'D-don't shoot, M-mister Norton,' he stuttered out. 'I give up. It were Pa's idea to lure you in here.' Desperation saw him offering up any excuse to save his own bacon. 'I-I didn't w-want no part of it. B-but they made me.'

Such was the kid's panic-stricken manner, he completely failed to appreciate that Rick's gun was empty. The gambler's deadpan regard gave nothing away. His gun remained steady as a rock. A face twisted into a rancid snarl was intended to strike fear into the young cowboy as he took a step forward.

'I ought to lay you out alongside those two miserable no-goods.' The abrupt threat hung in the hot air, leaving Billy Quindle visibly shaking in terror. 'But I don't shoot a man down in cold blood. That said, if'n I ever see your ugly puss around here again,

I'll gun you down on sight.' His voice rose in a throaty roar. 'You hear me, boy?' All the kid could manage was a fearful half-dozen nods of acquiescence. 'Then mount up and get out of here, pronto, afore I change my mind.'

Young Quindle couldn't exit Dead Horse Canyon fast enough. He never stopped until the border with Mexico had been crossed.

Meanwhile, the reality of just having killed two men struck home with a vengeance. The smell of death hung in the air. His gaze dropped to the sightless eyes staring blankly at the blue firmament. Alone once again, Rick pondered over the lives cut short. Never an easy task for someone who did not intentionally seek out trouble. Circumstances, the throw of the dice, had made him a pawn in the game of life, and death. But a man had to play the cards he was dealt.

He hawked a glob of spittle at the two corpses. They had it coming. Bushwhackers were the scum of the earth. Nevertheless, it didn't stop him wishing that life could be more accommodating, more benevolent. Gambling was a job, a way of earning a living. Gunfighting, however, had become a matter of survival; unwanted but hard to abandon.

With a sigh of acceptance as to what fate had tossed in his lap, Rick heaved the dead bodies on to their horses. He then gathered up the reins and headed back in the direction of Spindriff. A wide-ranging scrutiny probed the bleak terrain just in case Billy Quindle had gotten his nerve back. But no abnormal presence announced itself. The kid appeared to have been scared out of his wits, maybe having learned a valuable lesson.

Some time later Rick entered Spindriff with the aim of reporting the frustrated ambush and its grue-some aftermath to the law. His figuring was that he had only been protecting himself. So it came as a stunning shock to find himself being accused of murder. Cody Saggart was sympathetic to his claim of self-defence. But Elly had laid it on thick when expos-ing her ex-beau's avowed determination to take the law into his own hands.

Brad Quindle had also sowed the seeds of disquiet among his council colleagues following the gambling altercation by pressing his innocence in the matter. This had been communicated to Saggart in no uncertain terms owing to his friendship with the gambler.

'If'n you had a grudge against the Bar BQ you should have let me handle it,' the lawman declared. 'The days of playing the vigilante in Spindriff are over. That's the reason I was appointed marshal.' He held out his hand for Rick's gun. The accused man reluctantly complied. Saggart's stern regard momen-tarily eased. 'I feel for you, Rick. You had every right to be aggrieved. But I wear this badge with pride. I know we're friends, but duty has to come first. And I have no intention of letting you or anyone else ignore it.'

They were in the marshal's office. The door to the only cell was standing open. 'By rights I ought to lock you up,' Saggart murmured with some hesitation. 'But I'm gonna hold you to your word that you'll go and stay in my room at Maisy Jay's lodging house while I put your case to them. But you know how Harvey Rizzlock and those other turkeys feel about your presence in town. I can't promise anything.'

'Much obliged for your faith in me, Cody.' Rick was genuinely grateful for the old timer's belief in him. 'But you know that a fella in my position can't allow bums like the Quindles to lord it over him. He was a bad loser in that game, and tried to throw the blame on me.'

'Sure, I know that, Rick. But it's the way you always have to settle things in such a final way that scares folk. Gunplay only ever attracts the worst sort of approval. In my book it should only be called on as a last resort.' He ushered his friend out of the back door. 'Better not let anyone see you walking free until I sort this mess out.'

Two hours passed, with Rick nervously pacing the small room in the boarding house before that fateful knock on the door jerked him from his morbid ruminations. A curt summons to enter found Cody Saggart hesitant to deliver the result of his meeting with the council. The lawman's morose look told its own story.

'Might as well spit it out, buddy,' Rick said, his acidic tone chock full of biting mockery. 'What dire punishment have those mealy-mouths decided?'

'I did my best.' The lawman twirled his hat nervously. 'They were all set to have you up before the circuit judge on a charge of wilful murder. I told them about the ambush and that you were only defending yourself.'

'I guess that went down like a ton of bricks.'

'Thing is, I did manage to meet them half way by agreeing that you should leave town forthwith. It's the best I could do.' Saggart's manner stiffened on seeing the cold leer creasing his friend's face. 'You ain't gonna cause no trouble, are you, Rick? That would be a right foolish move.'

The gambler slumped on to the bed. 'Don't worry none, Cody,' he sighed, listlessly accepting the verdict. 'I'll go quietly. You go back and tell those turkeys they've seen the last of Rick Norton. I'll be out of their hair by sundown. That should make them happy.'

CHAPTER FIVE

BRUSH-OFF

And so it came to pass. But now the gambling gun-slinger was back. And he wanted answers. Yet it was clear as good beer these critters still harboured a grudge over an incident that had been rehashed to make him out to be the guilty party. Now it was the new tin star who was pushing his case with that darned council.

On this occasion, however, the entire town's future was at stake. Would Rizzlock and his cronies take Smokin' Joe McCabe's intimidation seriously?

Cody Saggart was the only one who had believed his claim of innocence before. Perhaps he could add some much needed weight to sway the critters his way. So focused was the gunfighter on his determination not to be pushed around, Rick failed to heed the rangy figure who had stepped out into the street and was now standing in his way.

'You and me have unfinished business, Norton.' The growled parlance snapped Rick from his reverie. It was a voice from the past. And one he instantly recognized. Absent when his kinfolk had been removed, Baz Quindle had now shown his hand and was plainly eager to settle the score.

'Guess you've already seen that open pit in the cemetery waiting on your mangy carcase. Well, I aim to fill it.' Rick pulled up short, studying Quindle's rigid figure. He didn't know it, but at the time of the disastrous incident in Dead Horse Canyon the elder Quindle brother had been visiting Tucson for the purpose of buying a prize breeding bull.

'I'm gonna count to three, then we go for our guns. Those other poor suckers should have taken you out in a proper fight. Baz Quindle aims to do the job properly.' He hunched down, right hand clawed and ready to reach.

'One. . . .' Both men stood facing each other, neither moving a muscle.

'Two. . . .' Quindle had advertised his intention of a showdown to all and sundry in the Blue Parrot. Those eager to see blood spilled were gathered on either side of the street, but removed from the line of fire.

'Th . . .' But before the deadline could be called, the challenged duellist strolled past the stunned hardcase, leaving him open-mouthed at the varmint's effrontery. But Quindle was prompt in recovering his shock at being denied revenge.

'Can't face a real man head-to-head, can yuh?'

Then to all those onlookers equally amazed by this unexpected climb-down by the alleged gunfighter, he called out for all to hear: 'That lowdown varmint has a yellow streak painted down his back. Don't be thinking this is the end of the matter, Norton. Make no mistake, I'll force your hand sometime soon. Then it'll be Baz Quindle who's cock of the walk.'

Rick struggled manfully to ignore the ranting tirade. All his instincts screamed out to wipe that smarmy grin off the cocky buzzard's kisser. Luckily, common sense won the debate. He followed the prudent advice of circumspection. No advantage would be gained by playing into this two-bit gunslick's hands and thus further alienating the powers that be in Spindriff.

That said, Rick was in no doubt that sooner or later he would have to meet Baz Quindle in a showdown. But it would be of his time and choosing. He continued down the street maintaining a straight course, back straight, shoulders squared, offering a silent helping of disdain to his tormenter.

All that Quindle could do was toss his head, mouthing off ineffectual insults to those within earshot. His moment of glory had passed, deflated like a punctured balloon. No way could he shoot a man in the back with plenty of onlookers around. That would be a certain road to perdition. Pushing the crowd aside he stomped up on to the boardwalk heading back to the Blue Parrot.

It so happened that Judd Farlow had been watching the proceedings with interest. He stopped the braggart in his tracks. 'Why didn't you gun him down?' the councillor demanded. 'The town doesn't need a dangerous critter like Norton free as a bird to walk the streets.'

Quindle scoffed at the notion. 'You saw how he reacted. The yellow rat couldn't face me man to man.' He spat in the dust. 'Next time we meet, though, I'll make certain he don't back off.'

Farlow gripped the swaggering firebrand's arm. 'Don't do anything without my say-so. Next time we need the conditions to be right. And with what I have in mind, he'll be so up tight, there won't be no stopping him drawing that six-shooter. Then he's all your'n.'

Farlow stuck a wad of banknotes into the cowpoke's shirt pocket. 'Get yourself a drink or two. And keep a low profile until I give you the word.'

The councillor's lofty manner irked Quindle, but he managed to contain any umbrage to a sour look. Since selling the Bar BQ to Farlow at a knockdown price due to his inability to run the spread as a going concern, Baz had become a mere hired hand. He might still be foreman, but that was a distinct climb-down from being the owner. And it was all down to that skunk, Red Spot Rick Norton.

'And when will that be?' snarled the surly jasper, still prickly from the sly obstruction to his plot of retribution.

'All will be revealed when I'm good and ready,' Farlow said knowingly tapping his nose. 'But rest assured, that fella is living on borrowed time.'

The man in question was at that moment pushing open the gate into a small, neatly kept garden. Flowers were growing on one side with ripening squash plants on the other. Green check curtains graced the windows of the small shack. Watching his old pal weeding the plot, Rick allowed himself a brief smile. It was clear that Cody had settled comfortably into a life of retirement. So involved was the ex-lawman, he failed to heed the arrival of his visitor.

Rick breathed deep before announcing his presence. The old-timer was going to have his carefree routine thrown into disarray when he revealed McCabe's malicious plan of revenge. But that could wait. No sense raising the alarm too soon. 'Looks like you got life all figured out, Cody,' he declared brightly.

The older man dropped his hoe. Startled out of his rapt concentration, he looked up. 'Well, I'll be darned, Rick boy!' A wide grin split the leathery contours. He was genuinely pleased to see his old friend. 'When did you hit town?' But then the beaming smile slipped. 'I'm sorry it had to be under these . . . erm . . . sad circumstances. We gave your pa a decent send-off. Most of the town turned out. Chester was well liked.'

Rick nodded his understanding. 'I went straight down to the cemetery to pay my respects.' He went on to outline his meeting with the new marshal and the grim reminder in the form of the empty grave openly flaunting the reason he had been forced out of Spindriff all that time ago. 'I've only been here for an hour. Yet already I've been refused service by Harvey Rizzlock, hissed at by Ma Huckarby, and called out by Baz Quindle.'

'You didn't . . .' Saggart gulped nervously as he butted in, eyes wide and fearful, knowing his young associate's reputation for blunt reprisals.

'No need to fear, Cody,' Rick assured his buddy. 'You would have heard the gunfire if'n I'd risen to his baiting. Not that I wasn't tempted mind you, after seeing what he left for me in the graveyard.'

'Folks around here have long memories. You know that. And you must admit, boy, you gave them plenty to worry about.' He gestured for Rick to follow him into the house where a bottle of Scotch was produced. 'To a bright future,' Cody proposed, raising his glass.

Rick hesitated to acknowledge the sentiment, pausing to gather his thoughts. A look of anxiety drew the skin around his mouth tight. Cody Saggart was not slow in noting a tense expression. 'Something else on your mind, Rick?'

'Guess there ain't no easy way of saying this, buddy.' He slung the glass of whisky down his throat. 'Smokin' Joe McCabe has escaped from the pen and is heading this way. He's leading a gang of hard-nosed gunmen and aims to rob the bank properly this time. And that ain't the worst of it.' A deep breath foreshadowed the grim tidings. 'He then intends burning the town to the ground.'

The retired marshal's crumpled features turned a darker shade of grey. He dropped the glass, which shattered on the floor. Some time was needed to get his head around such a momentous revelation. 'I'm gonna have to get the council together and organize some sort of resistance.'

'Blake already has that in hand,' Rick said. 'I've offered my help, but those critters may not be too keen on having a bad apple like me around.'

'How long have we got?' Saggart shot back, stroking his stubble-coated chin.

'I reckon they'll be here sometime tomorrow afternoon. And after my rather blunt refusal to join him, McCabe will be even more determined to have his revenge.' He briefly related the incident at the Raiders' camp. 'So while the council are making up their minds, I figure on paying Elly a visit. Does she still live with her folks out at the Jordan spread?'

A perfunctory nod was followed by some more disquieting news. 'She's running the place by herself since her folks died of a cholera outbreak six months ago,' Saggart paused before cautiously adding, 'with some help from Judd Farlow.'

Rick's thoughts were fully taken up by his forthcoming visit to his old sweetheart, otherwise he might have heeded the shifty expression clouding his friend's leathery visage. After finishing his drink he left soon after, and made his way back to where his horse was tethered outside the general store.

Cody Saggart was left with plenty to mull over. The grim news had badly rattled the old fella. Along with numerous others still resident in Spindriff he had helped ensure that Smokin' Joe was put away for a long spell in the pen. None of them could ever have foreseen that the outlaw would escape from the allegedly impregnable prison to wreak his revenge. It was a foregone conclusion that no mercy would be shown by the bandit leader to anybody who had had a hand in that sentence.

Unbeknown to their unwelcome returnee, the council were at that very moment voting on the thorny issue of whether he should be allowed to help them defend the town against the threatened incursion. Mayor Rizzlock along with his two main supporters, Lem Carney and Judd Farlow, had enough influence to sway those waverers who were undecided. And from the vehement arguments being tossed about, it was plain as a pikestaff that these three were against giving him a free hand.

The new marshal was the only one in favour of accepting Rick's help. 'We need a guy of his experience to tackle this gang,' he stressed. But Denny Blake was a relative newcomer. He had not been in the job long enough to have built up sufficient authority when important matters were under discussion. Rizzlock was quick to remind everybody of the reason for Rick's expulsion in the first place. 'He's too much of a hot head. We can't trust a guy like that.'

'And he'll be seeking his own form of revenge for being forced to leave in the first place,' Carney added with emphasis.

'My bet is that he'll turn that six-shooter against us when those critters make their move.' The forceful denunciation came from Judd Farlow, asserted firmly but with measured potency. 'Like as not he's a member of the gang sent here to suss out the opposition against them.' None of the others had considered that Norton could be in league with the Arizona Raiders.

That final accusation sealed the absent defendant's fate. The vote that followed was unequivocally in favour of Marshal Blake ordering Norton to leave town at the earliest opportunity.

'Sure I'll do that, boys,' the marshal declared while casually lighting up a cigar. 'He'll be out of your hair first thing tomorrow. I guarantee it. He even so much as fires that Colt revolver at a varmint, I'll clap him in jail faster than Lem Carney ducks out of buying a round of drinks.' That remark elicited a short-lived bout of hilarity.

'Hey, that ain't fair,' the banker protested. 'I pay my way.'

'Sure you do, Lem,' Reverend Coolidge scoffed cheerfully. 'Just like you always toss a dime in the church collection every Sunday thinking nobody's spotted you.' Even more mocking ribaldry greeted this well known dodge.

The marshal quickly brought the meeting to order. 'Let's get back to the problem in hand, gents.' A jaundiced eye panned the gathering of town officials before stating the one factor they had overlooked. 'So which of you fellas can I count on to help make a stand against the Raiders? Remember that most of those I could have deputized have up sticks and headed for that new gold strike at Turtle Creek. No amount of persuasion is gonna drag them back here to face a hornet's nest. And even if'n they do agree to help, it'll be too late by then anyway.'

Nervous, somewhat guilty looks passed between the seated councillors. Carney's discomfiture was forgotten as the truth of their situation hit home. This was yet another problem they had failed to consider. Feet shuffled uneasily as the seated men contemplated the thought of taking up arms. They were administrators, farmers and storekeepers elected to ensure the town ran smoothly. It was left to others, those more experienced in such matters, to protect them. Men such as Denny Blake and Cody Saggart.

Yet even with the threat of retribution hanging over their heads, nobody was ready to reverse the decision to ostracize Rick Norton. All of them had vivid memories of the hard-bitten contenders who had visited Spindriff hoping to encounter the renowned gunslinger, each hopeful of securing that coveted crown of thorns. Such spine-chilling recollections were hard to displace.

Rizzlock stood up, thumbs hooked pompously into his suspenders as he puffed out his chest attempting to play the doughty town superintendent. After all, wasn't it he who issued the orders? No thought was given to the fact that others did all the hard work. 'Norton is just one man. There must be enough fellas left to defend us against these brigands. It's your job to find them, Blake. That's what we pay you for.' Eager nods backed up this piece of truth.

71

Blake's chin jutted forward along with a prodding finger. 'Then I guess you'll be the first to offer your services, Mister Mayor. You being an upright and highly respected citizen and all.'

The weasel-faced mayor struggled to evade the challenge. But like all good posturing peacocks he had an answer for every occasion. 'I'm no gunslinger. I haven't even handled a weapon since I was a kid. Like as not I'd shoot myself in the foot.' There was no answer to that assertion.

Blake looked at the others, all struggling to avoid his accusatory gaze. 'What about you, Carney, this is your fight as well? And I've seen you out hunting in the hills. What's your excuse?'

The bank manager was likewise equal to the taunt. 'No need to be insulting. You are a single man with no family ties. I have a wife and two kids to protect. Just like these others around the table. You're going to have to look elsewhere, Marshal. I'm sure there are enough single men left in town willing to back your play.'

'I'd certainly be willing to help, Marshal,' Judd Farlow interjected, 'but I'm getting married soon. I have my future bride to think of now.'

A snort of disdain from the beleaguered tin star greeted this lame excuse. The scorn-riddled gaze that swept across the elected officials elicited some uncomfortable shuffling, but still nobody was prepared to step forward and bite the bullet.

'Looks like when the chips are down, you critters have shown your true colours. And yellow overrides

72

all others. In that case I suggest you all warn your families to gather in the church by this time tomorrow. That's about when this shebang is likely to blow up.' Then, bestowing a poignant sniff of contempt, the lawman swung on his heel and stamped over to the council office door.

Before he could leave, Rizzlock made to reassert his authority with a final demand. 'Be certain you escort that killer to the town limits, Marshal. And make it sooner rather than later.'

Blake stopped and slowly turned around. 'Seeing as how the fella put his neck on the line coming here to warn us about this raid, I ain't gonna force him out afore I'm good and ready.' Cold-eyed and menacing, he silently challenged anyone on the town's ruling body to voice their dissent. Nobody, not even the disingenuous mayor, made any comment.

The first person he encountered on leaving the council chamber was Cody Saggart. 'How did it go?' the retired lawman asked in a morose voice.

Blake shrugged. 'As you'd expect from those mealy-mouthed lowlifes. They don't want Rick Norton anywhere within fifty miles of Spindriff. And to add insult to injury, not a single one of the squeamish rats will help me defend the town.'

'Well, you can count on me,' Cody assured his colleague. 'And I know of a few others who ain't scared of a fight. There's Mace Tobin at the livery stable, for a start. I'll go see him now.'

'I appreciate your support, Cody. You're retired. You don't have to put your life on the line.'

73

Saggart gave the remark a mocking guffaw. 'I'd do it just to show those yeller dogs up for the gutless curs they are. How Elly Jordan can hanker after a critter like Judd Farlow is beyond my comprehension.'

'That's women for you,' remarked a philosophical Denny Blake. 'I'm just glad that my dealings with them are kept on a strictly business footing.' He aimed a sly wink at the old-timer. 'If'n you get my drift.'

The older man was not to be drawn into that kind of discussion. He was a God-fearing jasper and regular church-goer. 'Rick's gone out there to see her. He's in for a big surprise when he discovers her real intentions.' A quizzically raised eyebrow from Blake saw him filling in the critical detail: 'Those two were betrothed until his fall from grace.'

CHAPTER SIX

STARTLING REVELATIONS

Elly was tending her parents' grave when her unexpected visitor arrived. In truth, she had known in her heart that at some point during his homecoming Rick would be sure to pay her a call. And now that moment had arrived, she was dreading what it was she had to impart.

In a small town like Spindriff the unsettling news of his arrival was bound to reach her ears quickly. Evelyn Huckarby, being an incorrigible gossip, had made it her business to disclose the disquieting tidings. And it was clear as a church bell that the old gossip had relished the task even though she had assumed an outwardly disturbed face.

Rick joined her beside the headstone where she had just placed a spray of bright red poppies. 'I was sorry to hear about your folks', he began. 'Seems like we're both grieving at the moment.' A wan smile of appreciation from the girl was quickly replaced by a concerned frown she was unable to conceal. A woman's intuition told Elly the true reason for Rick's visit.

Since learning of her ex-sweetheart's return, she had puzzled over how best to break the fact that their past affair of the heart was just that. She had moved on and earnestly hoped that he had as well. The smile on her face was genuine enough. There was no doubt that seeing him here in the flesh evoked memories she had hoped to have buried. They had known each other since school days. And that could not be brushed aside. Nevertheless, their affair was over. And that was the way it would stay. She stepped out of the small enclosed burial site to greet him.

First, however, to welcome the handsome new-comer was Blue, the rough-haired deerhound, who instantly recognized this visitor from the past by his unmistakable smell. 'Good to see you, old fella,' Rick declared, rubbing the dog's shaggy head. 'It's been a long time. I've missed you heaps.' The smile lifted towards the main object of his visit, the salutation being for her benefit especially. 'You're looking real good, Elly. Just as I remember.'

'Nice to see you as well, Rick,' Elly said, forcing an upbeat brightness into her reception. He reached out to kiss her, but she quickly turned away offering a handshake in its place. The writing should have been on the wall, but Rick ignored the snub, so enthralled was he at seeing his lost love after all this time. She ushered him inside the house. 'The coffee has just brewed. And there are some fresh-baked cookies to go with it.'

That was when Rick began to sense the girl's reticence towards him. Their last meeting had been somewhat fraught following her warning about the Quindles. That said, he had hoped for a more congenial reception, a kiss on the cheek at least.

Once seated, Rick came straight to the point. He had never been one for smalltalk. 'Visiting Pa's grave was not my only reason for coming back here after all this time, Elly.' He put down his coffee cup and took hold of her hand. She did not pull away. 'I guess you must know that. It's true we parted on a sour note. But that wasn't my doing. Those durned Quindles forced my hand. I was left with no choice but to face them down.'

Elly quickly butted in. It was Rick's stubborn refusal to allow the law to take its course that had been the final straw in splitting them up. Her brusque rebuttal of his claim was scathing. 'There's always a choice, Rick. And you chose the wrong one. You should have left it for Cody Saggart to handle.'

Rick ignored the interruption. 'When I've finished here – and that could be mighty soon if'n the council has its way – I'm heading for California. There's a small orange farm out there in the Sacramento Valley that I've bought. All I need to make a success of the venture is to have somebody I can share my good fortune with.' The intimation was clear.

Elly tried intervening, but Rick's urgent plea brushed her reservations aside as he ardently pressed his case. 'We were always meant to be together, Elly. Ever since we were kids holding hands behind the schoolroom. Come with me. I promise to hang up my guns and consign them to history.' He took off his hat and removed the Queen of Hearts. 'And no more gambling.'

The girl turned her face away to hide the subdued, discouraging reaction to his proposal. She moved away to refill her coffee cup. 'So what do you say? Will you come with me?' The buoyant mood of anticipation reflected the positive response he clearly expected. It accordingly came as a disturbing jolt when she turned back to face him revealing a less than enthusiastic demeanour.

'Times have moved on, Rick. Three years is a long time. I've moved on.' The passionate suitor tried to intercede, but her raised hand cut short any protestation. 'You obviously haven't noticed this.' She held up her left hand. And there it was on the fourth finger, an engagement ring. 'I'm going to be married next month.'

He gulped, a knot of anguish strangling his guts. This was the last thing he had expected to hear. It felt like he had been kicked in the guts. Now it was his turn to stand up and pace the room. 'So who's the lucky jasper?' he asked struggling to maintain a coolly detached manner. 'I guess you have every right to turn me down. I ought never to have taken things for granted.' He headed for the door. This meeting

78

was plainly at an end.

'It's Judd Farlow,' she said trying to soften the blow to her old flame's wounded pride. Rick flinched, clutching at the doorframe. Judd Farlow – he might have known that critter would have wormed his way into her affections. 'You'll find a girl that suits you, Rick. Unfortunately it isn't me. A girl needs security, not a man who carries a reputation where the law of the gun takes precedence. I hope you won't hold it against me for choosing the safe option.'

'But I said I was willing to forsake all that,' he pleaded.

But the girl was unmoved. She turned away. 'Goodbye, Rick.'

It seemed like the final nail in the coffin of their liaison had been hammered home. A shrug of acceptance concealed the bitter disappointment he felt inside. Equally impossible to hide was the wave of torment written large across his blanched face. All the same he tried one last time to break down the barrier being erected between them. His voice rose to a final earnest supplication. 'A man can change, Elly. Ain't I proved that by going for the life of an orange farmer?'

'You might be able to,' the girl sighed shaking her head. The heart-rending look cast his way showed that Elly Jordan was truly sorry. 'But will others let you? I don't think so. You're too far down that trail to turn back now.' Her eyes dropped to the well-oiled gunrig strapped around his waist.

Rick's broad shoulders slumped as he accepted

the inevitable. 'Guess I should have known deep down that we couldn't just pick up the pieces and carry on. So if'n that's what you want, I hope you'll both be very happy together.' And with that he stumped out of the house, swung up on to his horse and rode off.

Back in Spindriff, Rick headed straight for the house at the end of the street. He needed answers from Cody Saggart. Why had the guy not warned him of the impending nuptials?

'I was hopeful that seeing you would change her mind,' the old-timer insisted when Rick confronted him. 'But it seems like I was wrong. I'm real sorry, boy.' He shuffled about clearing away some unwashed dishes, unable to meet his pal's potent gaze. The old-timer's easy-going manner had been replaced by a stilted, rather shifty posture. It was obvious to Rick that his old buddy was hiding something else.

'Out with it, Cody!' The directive for clarification was blunt and explicit. 'You haven't been square with me about Elly. So what else is there you ain't telling me?' Still the older man hesitated. But Rick was adamant. 'I'll find out from someone else. But I'd rather it was you if'n there's more bad news to hear.'

'Well,' the grizzled law veteran began hesitantly. 'Fact is ... your pa didn't die of a heart attack.' Saggart swallowed nervously. 'He was shot down in front of his own house. He must have heard the approach of horses outside and gone to see who had come visiting.'

The listener felt his head spinning and had to sit down. Bad tidings were hitting him thick and fast. First an open grave with his name on it, then a rejection from Elly, and now this. They say that bad news comes in triplicate. That saying sure had come to fruition for Red Spot Rick Norton. What more could befall the itinerant gambler? 'Better tell me the whole truth,' he muttered fastening a cold eye on the messenger. 'And don't spare me any of the details.'

'There ain't that much to tell,' Cody replied. 'I didn't tell you so you wouldn't go off half-cocked. They say it was marauders from over the border who shot your pa down. All on account of the dough he'd just borrowed to mortgage his property.'

Rick's eyes widened, his brow furrowing. Yet another eye-opening revelation. 'How much?' The demand came out rather more tartly than he had intended. After all, this wasn't Cody's fault. He was just the messenger.

'It was for five thousand dollars to improve the spread.' Cody shook his head in bewilderment. 'Lord only knows how they found out about it. I only knew because Chester told me in confidence. Your pa wanted to expand into pig farming and buy in a prize rooster to increase the egg-laying capacity of the hens.'

'So who else knew about the loan?'

'Only Judd Farlow as far as I know.' Cody scratched his head reaching for the whisky bottle. He poured them both a glass. 'It was him that made out the agreement and had your pa sign it. Carney at the bank was sceptical of the idea. He reckoned your pa was overstretching himself.'

Rick slammed a fist into the palm of his hand. 'I might have known that jasper was at the bottom of this.' His taut features hardened, a look of gritty resentment boding ill for the wily businessman. 'And it looks like he's buying up a lot more land around here, judging by the ownership signs I saw on my way in.'

'Ain't no doubting that Judd has done well for himself,' Cody agreed. 'He's even taken over as deacon of the church since your pa stepped down.'

'A regular Good Samaritan.' The acidic rejoinder was chock full of disdain. Rick was on his feet, the bunched fists eager to let fly.

Cody sensed the reckless abandon of rational judgement. The hot-tempered reaction that had got his buddy into trouble before was once again raising its ugly head. Hands laid on his friend's shoulders were meant to pacify the tensed-up frame. 'Now don't you go throwing out accusations without any proof, boy,' he stressed. 'Everybody in Spindriff thinks it was just that, raiders on the prod who stole the money, then disappeared.'

Rick ignored the suggestion. Once again it underscored his suspicions regarding Judd Farlow. 'You want proof? Then I'll find it. And the first thing is to take a look at that mortgage. Where is it held?'

'Over at the records office.' Cody's eyes lit up. 'And it just so happens that I still have a key. Rizzlock never asked for it back when I retired.' He went off to retrieve the vital means of access. 'Now that you've raised the issue, it makes me suspect some of Farlow's other acquisitions seemed perty dubious at the time. The guy has a slick way with him. Gotten folks eating out of his hand. You'll need to be extra careful how you handle this. Farlow has the council and the law on his side.'

'Don't you worry none. I ain't gonna do anything without due cause,' Rick assured the cautious ex-marshal. Although deep down, he had no intention of allowing Farlow to escape justice should his suspicions hold water. And Red Spot style meant gun law. 'Lead the way, Cody. I'm mighty keen to see this professed mortgage. I reckon it's too much of a coincidence for the dough to have been stolen so soon after it was acquired. Awful strange if'n you ask me. Things like that don't happen without somebody pulling the right strings.'

CHAPTER SEVEN

A WORSENING SCENARIO

The two buddies chose a circuitous route to effect a clandestine entry to the records office. They did not want any prying eyes or suspicious snouts delving into their covert enquiry. Cody advised his co-conspirator to hide down the adjoining alley until the coast was clear. Rick Norton was bound to attract too much unwelcome attention no matter how innocent his movements might appear.

Even so, it was still necessary to hang around some time and wait for the agreed signal. At that time of day there was an almost constant movement of people going about their everyday business. Rick was straining at the leash. His patience was pushed to the limit. All of his gambling acumen akin to playing the waiting game had to be called upon. On more than one occasion, he almost blundered out only to spot somebody crossing the dark entrance to the alley.

At long last it finally came. A low yet clearly audible owl hoot brought the unwelcome visitor scurrying out of hiding. Quickly the door was unlocked and the two men slipped inside, careful to lock up after them. Cody knew exactly where to find the all-important leather-bound ledger containing the mortgage deed. It was dark inside the room so they placed the ledger on the floor behind the clerk's desk. A candle was lit as Rick quickly thumbed through the various documents until he found the right one. Luckily they were all filed in date order.

'Here it is,' he hissed, hungry peepers scanning the official document.

And that's when he received yet another shock. All they could find regarding the transaction between Judd Farlow and Chester Norton was a bill of sale. 'This can't be right,' Rick exclaimed feverishly flicking through the various documents to ensure he had not missed the elusive mortgage. 'It's a Bill of Sale giving ownership of the farm holding to Farlow for the miserly sum of five thousand dollars.'

'I know that Farlow took possession of your spread soon after Chester was shot down,' Cody explained, patently baffled by this unforeseen development. 'This don't make no sense.'

'It makes perfect sense to me,' Rick snapped out, pointing to some marks at the top of the document. 'See that. Somebody has stuck another paper over this one. That must have been the mortgage. Pa's eyes weren't what they used to be. So he must have thought he was just signing for a loan, but Farlow duped him into handing over the farm.'

'Why, that two-timing shyster,' Cody railed. 'He's cheated your pa out of his land. I'd never have noticed if'n you hadn't pointed it out. So it must have been him that organized that raid to cover his tracks. But for your sharp eyes, nobody would ever have suspected a thing. We all took it for granted the deal was legitimate.'

Rick extracted the offending deed and stuffed it in his pocket before slamming the ledger shut. An icy glint reflected by the candlelight told Cody that his buddy had revenge in mind. And he knew exactly what that would involve. 'You watch your step, boy,' he cautioned. 'That critter has the law on his side. Don't be stirring up a hornet's nest that'll land you in the slammer.'

Red Spot Rick was good and mad. As far as he was concerned, the time for caution was past. Action was needed. 'I'm going out to the spread, the place that should still be my home. That skunk is gonna have to hustle up some serious explaining to wheedle his way out of this piece of treachery.'

Rick did not have long to wait before Judd Farlow arrived. He was sitting on the veranda smoking a cigar when the unwitting fraudster arrived. Tossing the butt aside, he stepped down to confront his adversary, not only in matters of the heart, but now as the instigator of his father's murder. He regarded the appearance of his rival with measured composure, a studied indifference. Gone was the burning need for instant retaliation. In its place, a quiet yet determined aim to achieve law-abiding justice as advised by Cody Saggart now controlled his actions.

Farlow dismounted, a smile coating his unctuous face. The wily businessman greeted Rick like an old friend. As a capable wheeler-dealer, he had no difficulty hiding any surprise at seeing the previous owner's son. 'Howdie, Rick. I was wondering when we'd meet up. Come to visit your old place?'

'Judd,' Rick nodded in return, striving to contain his resentment. 'It seemed the right thing to do under the circumstances.'

'I was real sorry about your pa dying like that so soon after he sold me the spread. We gave him a good send off.' The shallow condolences delivered, it was straight down to business. 'A meeting was convened and I regret to say that your visit to Spindriff has to be temporary. The council want to express their gratitude for warning us about McCabe's intended attack. But unfortunately the majority view was against you staying on.' He shrugged, ostensibly to convey his regret. 'I tried to sway them in your favour but they were adamant and want you out by tomorrow.'

'Well, that suits me just fine,' Rick returned brusquely. 'I have no wish to stay where I ain't welcome. And Elly made her view quite plain as well.'

'So she's told you about our plans.'

The mood between the two men was rapidly deteriorating. Rick's surly manner, the stiff posture and bunched fists hinted at an imminent confrontation. Farlow attempted to ease things down to a more amicable level.

'The old place hasn't changed much since you last saw it,' he said nonchalantly, gesturing for Rick to look around. 'But I've got big plans for the farm. As you can see, there's already a new barn and corral. Another couple of years and I'll have turned the place into the biggest cattle ranch in Pima County. Linked up with the Bar BQ, you won't recognize it.' His shoulder lifted in a thoughtless shrug as if it was of no consequence. 'Nobody can halt the wheels of progress, I guess.'

The false bonhomie was too much for the angry listener. 'Somebody can have a mighty good try. And that person is me.' Rick stepped forward to crowd the jasper. 'I'm on to your game, Farlow,' he rasped jabbing a finger into his chest. 'And you won't get away with it.'

For the first time the smile slipped, revealing the real Judd Farlow beneath. Yet ever the astute trickster, he instantly recovered his poise. 'I don't know what you mean,' he disputed hotly. 'I bought this place fair and square. Your pa sold me the land of his own free will for an agreed price.'

Rick snorted with indignation. He'd had enough of all this pussy-footing around. 'I know you hoodwinked him into thinking he was signing a mortgage deed when all along it was a bill of sale. Then you organized a raid to get your money back. And like as not it was you that fired the killing shot.' He hunkered down ready to draw his gun. 'Now you're gonna pay the ultimate price for your treachery.'

'I know you won't shoot an unarmed man, Rick,' Farlow declared, opening his coat. 'That ain't your style.'

The gunfighter hesitated. 'Maybe you're right at that,' he replied unfastening his gun belt. 'But there are other ways of getting at the truth.' He then walked across to his horse and laid the rig over the saddle.

Farlow walked up behind him still trying to assert his innocence in the matter. A warped leer souring the well-groomed persona betrayed the underlying deceit. 'You've got this all wrong, Rick. Can't we sort it out calmly like men of the world?'

But it was all a charade. As soon as Rick turned around, his adversary slammed a hard right fist into his face. The blow took Rick by surprise, sending him tumbling over a barrel into the dust. Straightaway Farlow stepped forwards, launching a savage kick at the fallen man's head. Had it connected that would have spelt the end of the tussle.

Rick had expected some sort of sly trickery from his opponent. All the same, the underhanded tactic caught him off guard. He managed to roll out of the way, scrambling to his feet. At the same time he shook off the mush caused by the devious strike. 'You'll have to do better than that, Farlow,' he snarled.

Following an initial display of prudent circumspection the combatants circled one another, each seeking an advantage over the other. It was Farlow who launched the first attack, diving in to secure a stranglehold on Rick's throat. Gritted teeth found him squeezing hard. Rick countered with a sharp knee jerk into the other man's groin, effectively breaking the fearsome hold.

Farlow grunted in pain. Now it was his turn to back away on the defensive. A right cross from Rick was parried as Farlow retaliated with a bruising fist in the stomach. And so it went on. But such ferocious grappling could not continue indefinitely without the participants tiring fast.

Both men were forced to pause, breathing heavily while each weighed up the other. 'I'll get the truth out of you,' Rick growled out. 'Then I'm gonna kill you.'

'You're on a loser there, Norton. I've already won over the girl and your spread,' Farlow sneered, carefully sizing up his opponent's movements. 'And the whole town's against you. Why not give up and leave while you have the chance? Baz Quindle is all set to gun you down if'n you try staying on.'

Rick's answer was a howl of rage as he threw himself forwards. Both men slammed against a garden fence, breaking it into matchwood. Over and over they rolled, crushing a flowerbed. Farlow was the first to break free and made a dash over to his horse. Rick scrambled to his feet and chased after the fugitive, grabbing him by the collar. 'You ain't getting away that easily,' he railed, tearing his adversary's shirt half off his body.

And there in front of the old Norton homestead,

the two rivals once again began trading blows. Back and forth they battled in the Arizona heat and dust, neither gaining any advantage to finish off his opponent. Rick was surprised by the resilience of the smarmy dude, whose fists he was struggling to prevent doing serious damage to his own body.

Beneath Farlow's outwardly sartorial panache lay a hard-boiled persona gained from his early years in the goldfields, where only the toughest could survive. He had soon discovered that only a tiny number of prospectors benefited from the riches to be accrued from digging out paydirt. After forking out ten times the normal charge for a jug of milk, the young miner saw where real wealth could be made. And with far less effort. His future prosperity was assured.

Rick was anxious to get this tussle over with. He began to press home his ruthless determination for retribution. Farlow was soon left in no doubt that he would lose a straight fight against this principled aggressor. The easy life had taken its toll. But he still had a few tricks up his sleeve. A handful of sand was scooped up and tossed into Rick's face.

Rick was forced to back off rubbing at his smarting eyes. The underhanded manoeuvre had left him stranded, unable to defend himself and allowing the artful braggart to snatch up a heavy fence post. Farlow hollered out a cry of triumph. A mean smile of victory saw him advancing, all set to deliver the knock-out blow to the bent figure. 'This is where you join your senile old man. And good riddance.'

Only the intervention of a woman's strident voice

prevented the brutal termination of the contest. 'Stop this at once, do you hear me?' It was Elly Jordan's arrival at just the right moment that prevented death or serious injury to her ex-beau. 'What's the meaning of this?' she berated the combatants, quickly leaping off her horse and placing herself between the two battlers. 'Engaging in a stupid fight like a pair of overgrown schoolboys. You both ought to be ashamed of yourselves.'

Torn shirts and bruised faces testified to the fierce clash she had interrupted. The sharp tongue-lashing from the woman whom each held in high esteem was indeed reprehensible. Neither could meet her derisive regard. 'Well? Is somebody going to explain?' Standing there, hands on hips like an irate school ma'am, Elly did not wait for a reply. Instead she addressed her concerns to Rick Norton. 'You haven't been back in the area more than a day and already you're causing trouble. Have you no shame?'

The object of her wrath had no intention of being browbeaten in front of his avowed rival. 'If'n you want the reason for this, ask your no-account betrothed,' he snarled, holding himself in check. 'I'm sure he'll have a basket full of excuses ready to dish the dirt on me.'

And with that final comment he mounted up and rode off. Elly now turned to seek an answer from her fiancé. 'So what was the fight all about, Judd? This isn't the kind of behaviour I expect from the man I agreed to marry next month.'

As predicted, Farlow was ready with an excuse that

laid all the blame on his rival. 'He's a sore loser, Elly. The jasper accused me of luring you away from him. He couldn't stand the fact that you chose somebody else. I tried reasoning with him. But you know Rick. He can't control his temper and was all set to gun me down. And would have done too if I'd been armed.'

Much to Farlow's delight, Elly's stony demeanour softened as she took his arm. 'I don't want you two fighting over me.' She gently chided her affianced. 'I'd like you to make it up with him, bury the hatchet. He won't cause any more trouble now he knows me and him are really finished.'

Farlow took her in his arms, once again the gallant amorist who had stolen her heart with his silver tongue and attentive manner. 'I'll do my best, darling. But it'll be down to him whether he accepts the olive branch.' Hopelessly captivated by the charm offensive, the girl then led him into the house to tend his injuries.

CHAPTER EIGHT

A PLAN
HATCHED. . . .

Night was beginning to draw in when Rick arrived back in Spindriff. It had taken the two-hour ride back for his nerves, if not his body, to finally settle. Suspicious looks from numerous quarters still came his way as he rode down the main street. But they had no effect, like water off a duck's back. He just glared back, forcing the oglers to look away. He was bruised and tired, and in need of a hot bath.

The brawl with Farlow had shaken him up, especially when Elly had been forced to intervene. If'n his chances of getting back into her good books were slim before, they had now been completely obliterated.

He nudged his horse over to the hitching rail outside the National Hotel where he was staying, and dismounted. So absorbed was he in his own despondency Rick failed to heed the group of rannigans lounging outside.

One of them stepped forward to block his way. 'You ready to take on a real man yet, backshooter?' The bluff challenge from Baz Quindle jolted the gambler out of his reverie. 'My gun hand is getting mighty itchy. And that grave still needs filling.' Quindle sniggered at his pals. 'Or is that rep of your'n all talk and no action?'

Rick's face set hard in a mask of irksome frustration. The last thing he needed at that moment was some gun-hungry jerk calling him out. He pushed the cocksure bragger aside without stopping. 'You fellas need to hog tie and brand this critter. He's been eating too much loco weed.' And with that acerbic brush-off, he went into the hotel leaving Quindle fuming and one of his buddies chuckling to himself.

'So you think this is funny, eh Boomer?' Quindle rapped out. 'Well, I don't.' And without any warning he slugged the offender with a hard right, sending the poor sap tumbling into the dust. Then he quickly stumped off, anxious to remove himself from the scene of his ignominy.

It was only later that evening that Rick finally recovered from the hard fought scrap with Farlow. His old buddy had applied a liberal dose of liniment to the cuts and bruises, along with some harsh words about demeaning himself by brawling with his adversary. 'Don't you reckon you're getting a bit too old for that?' Cody enquired while tending the injured man.

'He didn't give me any choice,' Rick protested. 'I only wanted some answers, and he decided to cut up rough.'

'Oh, sure,' replied the cynical ex-lawman. 'And I'm the man in the moon. I know you, Rick Norton. When your dander's up, sparks are bound to fly.' A dab of stinging iodine on a cut saw the gambler wincing out loud. Cody looked in the mirror admiring his own medical handiwork. 'Guess you're fit as you'll ever be to face your public. I've reserved us a table at Fat Nelly's Diner. And don't tell me you've lost your appetite. She still makes the best steak pie in the county.'

Half an hour later they were tucking in when Denny Blake joined them. 'I ain't staying,' he muttered somewhat diffidently. 'Fact is, the council overruled me. They want you out of town pronto. I stressed that you'd come here to warn us about the raid. But Carney was having none of it. He claimed the only reason you'd come back was to cause trouble. The others backed him up.'

Rick nodded. 'I heard all about it from none other than Judd Farlow in person.'

'Looks to me like you didn't take the news too well,' the marshal replied, staring at the diner's multi-coloured features.

'He's still alive if'n that's worrying you,' Rick smirked, forking a piece of pie into his mouth. 'For the time being, at least.' The remark produced a chuckle that evinced a cringing grimace.

This was not what the lawman wanted to hear. 'I don't want no trouble from you, Red Spot. I've got enough on my plate with McCabe's invasion without you making things worse.'

'Keep your hair on, Denny,' Rick assured the town marshal. 'Any more dealings with Mister Farlow will be carried out well beyond the town limits. That is if'n I ever manage to find the rat. He knows what to expect when I catch up with him next time.'

'Glad to hear it. I sure don't want to lock you up.' Blake took a breather, helping himself to a cup of coffee before continuing. 'Rizzlock was all for me escorting you to the county line tonight. I persuaded the council to hold off another day. But tomorrow noon has to be the deadline.' He shrugged. 'I did my best. But the weak-kneed critters ain't for shifting.'

'I appreciate your support, Denny.' Rick was genuinely moved by the lawdog's backing.

'Well, make sure you don't let me down. Any trouble and you'll be under arrest.' Rick nodded his compliance as Denny added, 'I'm going over to the Blue Parrot now to try convincing some jiggers to help defend the town. It'll be an uphill struggle with all the most likely candidates seeking their fortune at Turtle Creek. The town's gonna have to pay double the going rate for any deputies I do manage to hire. And should Rizzlock voice any complaints I'll hand in my darned badge. I ought to do that anyway. But my conscience won't let me.'

'Good luck to you, Denny,' Rick said. 'I only wish I

could be on the payroll.'

'Me too, Red Spot, me too.' And with a regretful sigh Blake walked out the front door. He failed to notice a pair of restless eyes that had been avidly watching the confab with ill-concealed hatred from a side alley window close to where the two diners were seated.

Baz Quindle drew his pistol. This was his chance to get rid of that leech once and for all. He waited until the lawman had disappeared into the saloon, impatience riddling his warped features. The gun rose to deliver its lethal charge.

Before he could pull the trigger, an urgent hiss behind stayed his hand. 'Don't be such a fool.' It was Judd Farlow. 'This isn't the way to have your revenge. I told you before that I'd let you know the time and place.'

'What better time than here and now?' the gunman remonstrated.

'I thought you wanted to become top gun in the territory?' Farlow declared as if he were speaking to an unruly child. 'You won't earn a reputation like that shooting somebody down from hiding. It needs to be in the open and in front of an audience.' He paused allowing the import of his logic to sink in. Quindle's need to save face had momentarily overruled his rationale. 'Keep a lid on that impatience until tomorrow. I'll set things up so that the Red Spot will have to draw on you.' Farlow looked the young hothead squarely in the eye. 'You can beat him, I take it?'

Quindle scoffed. 'Does a dog have fleas? I just need the chance to prove it.' His eyes misted over at the thought of what gunning down Rick Norton would mean.

'Then you wait on my call. Remember, tomorrow afternoon and not before.' Quindle drifted away dreaming of the dubious respect that would be his for the taking, the grim notoriety as the man who gunned down Red Spot Rick Norton.

Around the same time, Elly Jordan arrived in town. She also spotted Rick and his buddy at a table eating their supper. Entering the diner she walked across. 'Mind if I have a few words with you, Rick?' she said accepting a seat. As the meal was now finished, Saggart excused himself, knowing this was a discussion best left in the hands of those intimately involved.

Once they were alone Elly expressed her concern. 'I need to know what your fight with Judd was all about,' the girl declared stiffly. 'He said it was because you were jealous of me and him getting married.'

'Could be he had a point.' Rick's reply was measured, lacking any emotion.

'I think there was something more that you aren't revealing.'

'Maybe you should ask him about that.' Her probing inquiry was casually brushed aside. 'But I doubt you'll get a straight answer.'

Elly's brow furrowed in frustration. 'I'm not getting a straight answer from you, either.' Her voice hardened to a snappy rasp. 'Why can't you be open with me?'

'You've made your choice, Elly.' Even though he now accepted their romance had long since withered on the vine, he still did not want to appear churlish by telling her the awful truth about her future husband. She would have to find that out for herself. 'It's not for me to judge how you choose to live your life.'

'Well, if that's all you have to say, I guess I'm well rid of you,' she retorted standing up.

'Reckon you are at that,' came back the equally terse rejoinder. It was not a pleasant way to end a meal. But Rick was not in the mood to be considerate. He was being hounded out of Spindriff once again for no good reason. A morose feeling of animosity towards the town and its bigoted inhabitants made him glad to be purging them from his life. Come the following afternoon, he would be riding out.

And to hell with the lot of them.

He threw down a wad of dough to pay for the meal and stamped out. The hostile eyes of other diners followed his every step. They were ignored. The number of people he would miss could be counted on one hand.

Elly left soon after. Her brow was furrowed in contemplation following the recent unpleasant confrontation. As such she failed to heed Judd Farlow's approach. 'Hold up there, Elly,' he said stopping her. 'Why such a hangdog expression? We're getting married soon. You should have a spring in your step.'

'It's this threat facing the town,' she replied not wishing to discuss the real reason for her despondency.

'Don't you fret none, honey,' Farlow assured her. 'Now that we have advance warning, Marshal Blake will make sure the town is kept safe.' He peered hard at his detached fiancée. 'You sure there isn't something more bothering you?' He had spotted Elly emerging from the diner and suspected who she had been to see.

The girl had known Rick Norton most of her life. She knew that Rick was hiding something from her. And it had a lot to do with her fiancé. Elly had heard rumours about Judd's business dealings. But love conquers all. And she had brushed any qualms she might have harboured under the carpet.

Maybe she had been bowled over by his silver tongue, not to mention the frequent gifts culminating in that dazzling engagement ring. All her friends had been green with envy. Rick's return had thrown her expectations of a comfortable life with all the trimmings redolent of success into a maelstrom of wavering hesitancy. She needed time to sort through her emotions before making a lasting committal.

'I promised to help the pastor's wife get the church ready for all those people who'll be cramming in there tomorrow.' It was a spur-of-the-moment excuse to relieve herself of any more questions she was loath to answer. 'She's expecting me.'

Elly moved away quickly, leaving Farlow less than happy with the situation. That damned gambler could spill the beans about how the Norton holding was really acquired. The sooner he destroyed the evidence the better. He had a key. So there was no time like the present. A quick look around to ensure he was not being observed and he slipped into the Council Records Office.

Panic gripped the charlatan when he discovered no sign of the incriminating document. Much as he shuffled through the files, it was not to be found. Farlow let out a rabid curse of frustration. Norton must have somehow acquired the deed of sale. And he had put two and two together and come up with the right answer regarding the mysterious mortgage. It was now imperative that his scheme to get rid of the interfering troublemaker should be brought to fruition without delay.

After he had left Fat Nelly's, Saggart ambled over to the saloon where he found Denny Blake struggling to convince the patrons that the town needed their support if it was to survive. Every argument he could conjure up was being earnestly relayed to the idling throng, all of whom were less than enthusiastic. The old and infirm mingled with loafers and drifters. It was abundantly clear that all the able-bodied men had vamoosed to try their luck at the gold strike.

Yet still he managed to coerce a handful of weary souls into lending their guns in defence of the town, supported by the retired lawman. A deputy's fee would buy a heap of booze. 'First thing in the morning we'll construct a barricade across the north end of Main Street,' he announced. 'McCabe and his gang will be coming from that direction.'

Just then the door of the saloon was pushed open and two strangers entered. They sauntered over to the bar and ordered a couple of beers. A pair of shifty roughnecks clad in rough trail gear, Blake eyed them up suspiciously. 'You boys come far?' he casually asked.

The larger of the two, Wolf Maddigan, was a bulky jasper sporting a ragged black beard. A knife scar over his left eye gave him a lupine slant that merely added to the roughness of his appearance. After taking a large gulp of his drink, a satisfied sigh issued from the gaping maw. 'Gee, did I need that.' The man could not meet the lawman's penetrating regard.

'I asked you a question, mister.'

'We've come from Casa Grande up north,' the second man replied. Weasel Egger was smaller than his buddy, but the shiny revolver strapped low on his hip was no less conspicuous. 'Figured to hang around here a few days before heading across country to that gold strike on Turtle Creek.'

'You fellas don't look much like miners to me,' the marshal said, his cynical appraisal clearly scrawled across his face.

'That's because we're new to this game,' Maddigan shot back. 'Cow punching don't pay enough so we figured to try our luck at prospecting.'

'Which way did you come?' asked Saggart, who had wandered over. The old-timer's practised assessment of these two drifters had immediately put them down as gunmen on the prod. They weren't regular cowhands, that was for sure. Well kept shooters strapped down like that gave them away. 'Over Sentinel Pass and across the Sand Tank?' Saggart added casually. The man nodded absently. 'You must have called at Baxter Springs trading post then. How's Ed doing these days? I ain't see him for a couple of months.'

'The place seems to be doing good business,' the big jasper replied. Saggart gave the reply a sagacious nod. 'Glad to hear it. You fellas would do well not to stick around here, though.' Both men eyed him askance. 'A gang of villains are headed this way and they're aiming to burn Spindriff to the ground. Ever hear tell of a hellraiser named Smokin' Joe McCabe?'

'Ain't everybody?' the little fella drawled, effecting far less surprise at this startling revelation than would normally have been expected. 'They say that he's one mean cuss. Guess we'd better make tracks, Wolf. Don't want to get on the wrong side of that rannie.'

Now the conversation about the real reason for the two owlhooters' presence in Spindriff had come to a close, Wolf Maddigan nonchalantly enquired if they were ready for the attack. 'We'd offer to lend a hand, marshal, if'n you were short-handed. But this ain't really our business.'

'No need to anyhow,' Blake assured them. 'The

town has enough men and guns to blast McCabe and his bunch to Kingdom Come. He's in for the surprise of his life figuring Spindriff is gonna be a pushover.'

Maddigan and his little buddy failed to conceal the look of surprise on their leathery faces. 'Good luck to you then, Marshal,' the burly tough stuttered out. 'Be seeing you.' And with that the two men quickly left the saloon.

Blake watched the two mysterious visitors ride off, noticeably in the same direction they had arrived from. He was joined by Saggart. A cunning smile was all that betrayed the confirmation of his suspicions. 'Reckon we're both agreed on where those two critters are headed,' Blake remarked.

'They shot themselves in the foot by claiming that Ed Baxter was still in business,' Saggart added. 'He's been dead for years. There's only a lone cross to mark his passing now. And those shiny revolvers were also a dead giveaway.' The two men chuckled to each other.

But Blake knew what he was facing. And his next remark was tempered with caution and a stoical acceptance of the inevitable. 'Don't be thinking that McCabe will change his mind. Nothing is gonna turn him aside now he's come this far. That critter never gives up. And I'm the one he's gunning for, seeing as it was my testimony that sent him to Yuma in the first place.'

'At least figuring he has some stiff opposition to overcome will give the skunk something to chew on.' The old guy's square-cut chin jutted out, a mannerism affirming his resolve to resist any assault on the town. 'Give us the chance to put up some serious opposition.'

The new lawman slapped his associate on the back. 'It's mighty heartening to hear somebody talk tough for a change instead of bellyaching all the time.'

'Reckon we need a slice of luck,' Saggart concurred as the two men walked back into the Blue Parrot. 'And we're gonna need a whole lot more when McCabe turns up.'

They were immediately accosted by Lem Carney, who was worried by Saggart's claim that the town was well protected. 'What's all that hogwash about having plenty of men and guns to protect the town? Why didn't you tell those fellas the truth? That all the best men are away digging for gold.'

Blake responded with a stinging rebuke. 'You and those other wet blankets on the council ain't helping the situation by refusing to back me up. You may not know it, but those were two of McCabe's men sent here to suss out the opposition.' The lawman's eyes crinkled with satisfaction on seeing the banker's look of surprise. 'By spinning them a false tale, he'll be far more careful and that should give us, or me rather, the chance to mount a half-decent challenge.'

Blake ignored the simpering banker, and once again called for more volunteers to swear in. This time a few more men came forward. It wasn't anything like the number or quality of support he would have preferred. But beggars can't be choosers. The old, infirm and general wasters were better than nothing, just so long as they were sober and could shoot straight.

'Much obliged, boys, I appreciate your help. We'll meet up tomorrow morning behind the livery stable.' His appreciation was genuine. These fellas were putting their lives on the line. 'Some practice shooting before building a barricade across the street will come in handy. And bring every gun you can muster.' His next order, brusquely cutting and laced with disdain, was aimed at Harvey Rizzlock who was skulking behind a pillar. 'And I'm sure the mayor will buy you all a drink for being such good citizens.'

Cheers erupted from those men who had volunteered as they made a rush for the bar. Rizzlock squirmed in his seat but could do nothing but concur.

'And while these men are helping defend you and your families, Mister Bank Manager, I suggest that before noon tomorrow, you herd the rest of the town inside the church and keep them there. We can only hope and pray that Smokin' Joe will leave the House of God alone. And I can tell you, it's a mighty slim hope. So I suggest you pray like you've never prayed before.'

CHAPTER NINE

. . . ANOTHER SCRATCHED

Joe McCabe was not the only one peeved at having been bested by the Red Spot gambler. Other gun-happy desperados scattered from the Mexican border north to the Grand Canyon would have relished knowing his whereabouts. One of these, a hard-boiled redneck going under the bizarre handle of Hatchet Mag Luffrey, had struck lucky in Holbrook where the name of Red Spot Norton had cropped up during a poker game in the Sundance Saloon.

Hatchet Mag had earned his grizzly name from an equally hideous penchant for chopping up his victims into pieces, then allegedly eating them. The former was certainly true. As to Luffrey's cannibalistic tendencies, no evidence had ever emerged. But that didn't prevent the myth from swelling with each narration as Luffrey helped it along.

The villainous rogue had a particular reason for seeking out his quarry. Rick had shot down his young brother on the streets of Farmington, New Mexico, when the kid had called him out. It had been a fair fight, but Hatchet Mag did not choose to see it that way. And he had boasted that Norton's carcase was going to be spit roasted and fed to the coyotes.

A surreptitious enquiry had found Luffrey heading south, tracking his quarry to Spindriff, where he arrived late that day. With daylight fading, his arrival had passed unobserved by those whose only thought was of the coming attack on the morrow. The newcomer had booked into the National Hotel under the name of Elmer Tripp, a travelling salesman.

A rubbery face enabled the crafty crook to alter his demeanour at will. False whiskers, a moustache and spectacles, as the occasion required, had enabled Mag Luffrey to evade the long arm of the law for many years. He could certainly give the wily chameleon a run for its money. Indeed, only a particularly assiduous inspection of those darkly hooded eyes chock full of malice and evil intent could betray the true nature of the hatchet-wielding brigand.

Slick chat akin to that of a vaudeville comedian provided Luffrey with the vital information that Rick Norton was staying in room number 5 on the first floor. 'I will certainly make sure to give that fellow a wide berth during my stay in your good town,' the bogus salesman espoused, assuming a timid manner.

'You'd be well advised, Mister Tripp, to get your business here in Spindriff over quickly,' counselled the desk clerk.

'And why is that, my good man?'

Luffrey was visibly startled by the clerk's unexpected revelation: 'We're expecting an attack by Smokin' Joe McCabe and his gang. They've threatened to rob the bank and set fire to the town. Reliable proof has been furnished that he will be here some time tomorrow.'

Luffrey's eye-popping display was no piece of theatre.

So McCabe's bunch were close by. This news could most certainly work to his advantage. Get rid of Norton tonight, then light out and wait on the marauders' arrival and offer his services. For a suitable cut of the proceeds naturally. 'Much obliged for the timely suggestion, sir,' he said, accepting the key to his own room.

It was Number 6, right next door to his quarry. Perfect. Luffrey tried not to show his satisfaction, affecting a nervous croak. 'It's a bit close for comfort, being housed next to that villainous rogue,' he whined. 'I trust it has a lock.'

'It certainly does, sir. No chance of a break-in, I can assure you.' The bogus drummer nodded, accepting the situation with studied grace.

Once in his room, Luffrey threw himself on the bed. Curbing an impatient streak was hard for the killer. But the result would most definitely be worth

the wait. Not until the clock downstairs chimed mid-
night did he deign to make a move. At that hour all
was quiet.

The prowler noiselessly slipped out of his room
and tiptoed along to the next room. An ear to the
door of number 5 revealed silence within. Luck was
also on Luffrey's side with number 5 being an end
room with a window facing on to an outside veranda.
He stepped outside. The sash was partly open to
allow cooling air inside. Another windfall. His hand
strayed to the lethal axe tucked into his belt.

The shaft of the Comanche tomahawk was intri-
cately carved. It had been taken from a dead brave
who had tried and failed to bury it in Luffrey's body.
The lone renegade had made the mistake of attacking a man armed with the latest Henry repeating
rifle, and was easily taken down with a single bullet.
So impressed was the new owner with both the
balance and razor-sharp honing of the curved blade,
that he decided to adopt it as his own weapon of
choice for silent and meaningful terminations. The
grim talisman had never let him down.

He hefted it now while gently peering through the
window of room number 5. An eager smile, cold and
malicious, fastened on the still form on the bed. The
guy appeared to be firmly in the land of nod.
Unfortunately for Hatchet Mag, the intended recipient of his noxious ally had developed the knack of
sleeping like a cat. The slightest distraction and he
was instantly awake. It had saved Red Spot's skin
before. And the brief yet significant creak as the sash

window rose found the reposing gunfighter stirring as he listened carefully.

There it was again, another creak. He remained absolutely frozen, all senses now on the alert. Somebody was most definitely attempting to enter his room, and unobtrusively, which intimated skulduggery with his continued good health at risk. The problem – how to deal with it?

His revolver lay at the far side of the room slung over a chair, and beyond reach. Eyes attuned to the darkness picked out the silhouette of a crouched figure clambering silently through the window. And he was holding a tomahawk.

Rick's probing gaze focused hard as recognition dawned – Hatchet Mag Luffrey! The jasper had finally tracked him down and was intent on revenge for his kid brother's folly. Although his nerves were stretched tight as banjo strings, Rick knew he had the edge, with surprise his collaborator.

Slowly, step by step, the intruder crept across to the bed, the deadly tomahawk raised to deliver a bone-crunching strike. Rick needed to get his timing just right. Luffrey paused, looming above the apparently comatose victim. A hideously lurid beam of light revealed a row of warped, tobacco-stained teeth: the moment for which he had waited a full year had finally come to its execution – an appropriate word to describe what was about to be enacted.

The deadly blade fell, its inexorable course of mortal destruction now unstoppable. Instantly he saw the movement, Rick swivelled his body away.

The tomahawk whistled past, burying itself in the empty flock mattress inches from his body. No time was wasted in futile denunciation: he grabbed the hand gripping the handle and flung the killer aside. A startled howl of anger erupted from the open maw as Luffrey slammed back against the outer wall.

But the avenger was not beaten yet. He still had his revolver, which he dragged from its holster. But in the moment that followed Luffrey's thwarted ambition, Rick had taken hold of the abandoned tomahawk, which he now wielded to deadly effect. Flying end over end like a spinning wheel, the gleaming point ploughed into skin and bone. It stuck there, wedged tight in the rib cage with blood pouring from the fatal wound.

Hatchet Mag tottered, having swallowed the contents of his own poison chalice. His disintegrating body swayed. Weakening muscles were unable to tug the blade free. Rick watched as the failed exterminator slid to the floor having breathed his last. The intended victim slumped on to the bed. Heart beating twenty to the dozen, he shook off the traumatic consequences of the brutal assault, thankful that no shots had been fired. And just as relieved that none of the other hotel guests appeared to have been disturbed.

'So what to do now?' he muttered under his breath, casting bleak glances towards the grizzly result of the death-dealing encounter. The body had to be removed before morning. If Denny Blake found out, the lawman had given him due warning of the consequences. It mattered not a jot that once again he was blameless.

The only person he could trust to help him spirit the dead man away was Cody Saggart. Without further ado, he got dressed and sneaked down the back stairs. Hustling behind the back lots in the pitch black without causing a rumpus took some time. Cody's house was also in darkness. He went round to the rear and knocked on the back door.

A second louder rap produced a garbled imprecation as the ex-lawman's turgid brain struggled to formulate what had awoken him. 'Who in blue blazes is out there causing a hoo-ha at this time of night?' the roused sleeper gurgled.

'It's Rick. Let me in. I need your help pronto.'

The restrained hiss found Saggart scrambling out of bed and opening the door. 'What's going on, boy? You look like you've seen a ghost.'

'You ain't far wrong there, buddy,' Rick replied nervously looking around. 'Let me in and I'll tell you.'

Saggart ushered him inside. 'So what darned trouble have you caused now?' The cynical accusation was met with a spirited denial as the nightjar quickly related his recent fracas with Hatchet Mag Luffrey. Thick lines of concern ribbed Saggert's brow as the implications stacked up.

'We need to hide the body,' he asserted gritting his teeth. 'And I know just the place where nobody will find it in a million years. There's an old abandoned mine a mile out of town. We can drop it down the shaft. Ain't nobody ever going to venture in there.'

The wheels of concealment were quickly set in motion. There was no time to lose. A wagon was drawn up behind the hotel. Both men were needed to carry the blood-stained corpse quietly down from room number 5. A yowling cat dashing out from beneath the boardwalk set their nerves on edge.

'I'm getting too danged old for this kinda game,' Saggert muttered. 'Anyone else but you and I've have shopped 'em to Blake.'

Rick smiled through the turbid cloak of darkness. 'Ain't that what bosom buddies do for each other? There's nobody else in the town I could have called on.'

'Guess not. But it sure ain't good for my old ticker,' Cody grumbled good-naturedly returning the smile. A barking dog brought them back to the task in hand. 'Best get moving. Sooner we dispose of this fella the better.'

That was when Rick thought of a further problem. 'A new guest moved into the room next to mine sometime after dark. I'm figuring it was Luffrey. That means all his gear is in there. We'll need to dump that as well to give the impression he quit the hotel in the early hours to avoid paying. You wait here while I go back.'

Much as he was loath to return to the scene of the killing, Rick knew it was essential to remove all evidence of the grim deed. He could clean up his own room once Luffrey's presence in Spindriff, and his own complicity in the man's disappearance, had been erased.

CHAPTER TEN

HOODWINKED!

A full bottle of whiskey had been sunk following the elimination and disposal of Mag Luffrey. Both of the reluctant conspirators felt the need to expunge the macabre reminder, if only for a few hours. Next morning it was a loud hammering on the door of room number 5 at the National that jolted a hung-over Red Spot Norton back into the land of sobriety. His head was throbbing worse than an over-taxed steam engine. He turned over, burying his head in the bedclothes.

'You can't ignore the inevitable for ever, Rick,' the gruff voice of Denny Blake barked. 'It's noon, which means the deadline for your eviction. Now shift your ass, buster, afore I break down the door.' A pain-wracked bout of groaning on the far side was sufficient to inform the marshal that his demand had been heeded. 'I'll wait for you down in the lobby. Don't be long!'

Rick struggled into his clothes, then doused his

face with cold water. It went some way to alleviating the effects of too much hard liquor. Old Ma Huckerby would have a field day if'n she could see him now. He peered in the mirror. What stared back looked like it had been dragged across a ploughed field. But a few cups of coffee and a good breakfast would soon change that, then hopefully he would be good as new, or near enough, to ride out of Spindriff with his head held high.

Down in the lobby, he couldn't help noting the concerned frown cloaking the face of the desk clerk when he paid his bill. 'Some'n troubling you, mister?' he enquired casually.

The man was none too happy, that was for sure. 'A man who booked in last night has upped and skedaddled without paying. He seemed such a harmless fella, the kind that wouldn't say boo to a goose.'

Rick gave a nod of commiseration. 'You can't trust nobody these days.' Then he turned his attention to the hovering lawman. 'Mind if'n I have a late breakfast before you kick me out of town?'

'I'll join you,' was the cynical rejoinder. 'So that I know the job's been done.'

It was one o'clock outside the jailhouse before Rick was finally set to leave. It was a poignant moment, as history repeated itself. He looked around, somehow hoping that Elly would appear, begging him to take her with him. No such luck. All he saw was Harvey Rizzlock and Lem Carney watching from a distance. And there was no sign of Judd Farlow. No surprise there. Shoulders square, back

118

straight as a ramrod, he had no intention of giving these critters the satisfaction of seeing him depart in a subdued manner.

Denny Blake's good wishes were acknowledged with a brief nod. A firm handshake was reserved for his old pal Cody. 'You take care of yourself, Rick,' the old-timer said. Then in a whisper meant for no other ears. 'What you aiming to do about Farlow?'

Rick gave an apathetic sigh of frustration. 'Not much I can do now. The varmint's gone to ground. Scared to face me in a proper showdown. Anyway you better join the others on the barricade. McCabe will be here soon. And make sure to give him hell. Don't make it easy for the bastard.'

A final adios and the exiled Red Spot nudged his horse towards the edge of town. Rounding a corner on the approach to the church, he spotted a familiar figure nonchalantly leaning against the side of a building. And it was none other than Judd Farlow. The crooked dealer was the last person he had expected to meet out in the open. He had figured the rat was skulking in some corner, only to emerge after his departure.

'Decided to face me like a man, eh Farlow?' He drew his horse to a halt opposite his nemesis. 'I never thought you'd have the guts.'

'You've got me all wrong,' Farlow replied in an even tone. 'I only want what's best for the town. And for Elly not to judge me harshly. If you want justice for your pa's demise and I'm the scapegoat, then so be it.' He mounted up, the two adversaries riding off to face their destiny.

Passing the church, the sound of hymn singing accompanied by the organ reached their ears. Rick was all set to voice a scathing comment about cowards and yellow bellies renouncing their obligatory duty when a lone figure in black stepped out from behind a tree. It was Baz Quindle. 'Time's up, Red Spot. You can't back off now. So get down and face me like a man.' The challenger flexed his fingers ready to draw.

Straightaway Rick knew that he'd been set up by Farlow. A look cold enough to freeze the desert wind made no impression on the sly manipulator. Yet still Rick was loath to engage in a shoot-out right in front of the church. He turned his attention back to the cocky challenger. 'Just let me pass on my way, Quindle. I ain't got no beef with you.'

'This ain't for you to decide,' the angry hothead railed. 'Gunning down my two brothers and stealing my gal sealed your fate long ago. And there's still that empty grave to fill. Now step down and draw, you yellow rat! Or I'll gun you down anyway.' Rick sighed. He needed to disarm this critter pronto before any blood was spilled and, as usual, he got the blame. Stepping down off his horse, he kept his hands wide.

The ugly smile on Farlow's face slipped. This was not how things were meant to pan out. Ever the devious schemer, however, he quickly revised his plan.

Quindle's ugly smile of satisfaction was instantly replaced by one of horrified shock as he staggered back, clutching at the two bullet wounds in his chest.

The unsuspecting victim was given no time to ponder over the grim circumstances as death came a-calling.

But the killing shots had not originated from the arm of Rick Norton. Momentarily stunned by this sudden development, the hoodwinked dupe was likewise given no time to figure out the trap into which he had been lured. The barrel of the perpetrator's gun butt struck him hard on the back of the head. Rick went down like a sack of coal. And stayed there.

Both he and Baz Quindle had been well and truly suckered, though one had paid the ultimate price. And the other would soon follow if Judd Farlow played his cards right. The charlatan wasted no time in sanctimonious applause of his odious scheme. Those shots would have been heard by the congregation. Slipping off his horse, he quickly slotted his own still smoking Colt into Rick's hand, whilst holstering the inert man's gun.

And just in the nick of time, as the church emptied to determine the cause of the shooting. 'What is going on here?' enquired the minister leading his startled flock. Gasps of shock emerged from a myriad throats as the body of Baz Quindle was spotted. 'Is he dead?' stuttered the nervous reverend, as Doc Pilger examined the body. A nod confirmed the awful result.

That was when Lem Carney noticed the supine form of Rick Norton lying on the ground close by. The floored man was just coming to, unable to comprehend the enormity of what had befallen him. 'His gun is still smoking,' the bank manager observed, pointing at the macabre evidence. It was obvious to all what had occurred.

And it was left for Judd Farlow to gloomily relay the macabre circumstances. 'I followed Norton out of town to make sure he left without causing any more trouble. Quindle was coming the other way, and Norton forced him to get down and face him in a shoot-out. Quindle refused. So Norton just shot him twice in cold blood. I managed to stun him with my revolver while he was still standing over the body.'

At that moment Marshal Blake arrived and hauled the alleged killer to his feet. 'I gave you fair warning, Rick,' he snapped clamping the accused in hand-cuffs. He then sniffed the killing weapon. 'Two bullets just recently fired.' It was clear as daylight to all within hearing range that Rick Norton had finally succumbed to what was expected of him. 'You're under arrest for wilful murder. This is a hanging offence, Rick. Now shift your ass.'

'It's all a frame-up, Denny,' the accused man protested. 'I didn't shoot Quindle. He called me out, but I refused to draw.'

Blake was in no mood for empty denials. 'All the evidence is against you, Rick. You should have kept going and not given in to your natural instincts.'

That was when Rick noticed Elly standing forlornly on the edge of the hostile crowd. 'This ain't my doing, Elly,' he called out. 'It's Farlow that's fitted me up good and proper.'

The blank expression on the girl's face told him that the appeal had fallen on deaf ears. But Elly was deeply troubled. She had not failed to heed the sly smirk warping her fiancé's face during the arrest. He walked over and tried to link arms. Elly pushed him away. 'What is it, honey? Why so offhand? Norton has proved he's nothing but a killer at heart.'

His startled reaction brought a stern look from the girl. 'He said that it was all a frame-up by you.'

'What did you expect?' Farlow replied calmly. 'The man is a born liar and doesn't care who he hurts.'

'That isn't the Rick Norton I know. I thought you were going to settle things amicably between you both.'

'I tried, but he just wasn't for listening, as you saw just now.' The crafty smooth talker figured he had all the answers. 'He would have killed me as well after Baz Quindle if the congregation hadn't come out of the church.'

This time, Elly was less inclined to concede. Turning up her pretty nose, she replied, 'I need time to think this over, Judd. There's something you're not telling me. Maybe I've been taken in by your charm for too long.' Farlow's look of hurt innocence, the raised eyebrows, elicited a sniff of indecision as the girl walked away.

As for the wronged object of their troubling discourse, Rick knew that he had been pushed into a black hole. Extricating himself from such a tight spot would need a miracle. The walk back down the street was anything but a pleasant stroll. Pushing and prodding soon escalated into punches as the mood of the crowd became fractious. None of them harboured any liking for the dead man. But they were frightened, the killing of Baz Quindle had made them all more aware than ever of the danger they would be facing in a few hours time.

Blake struggled manfully to keep his prisoner safe as threats of vigilante law loomed heavy in the fetid air. 'Hang the bastard now!' from one irate citizen. 'We don't need a trial. He's guilty as hell,' another espoused vehemently. They surged towards the lawman and his tethered prisoner.

'There'll be no vigilante law in Spindriff,' Blake rasped, fending off the panicking throng. His raised gun was a compelling threat should the furore escalate. 'Norton will receive a fair trial according to territorial law. And anybody who tries to interfere with the due process will answer to me.' He pumped a couple of bullets into the air forcing back the angry mob, who moments before had been avidly praying for deliverance inside the church.

It was, therefore, with much relief when he was finally able to slam shut the door of the cell and turn the key. 'Much obliged, Denny.' Rick was genuinely grateful to have escaped with only a few bruises. 'Last thing an innocent man needs is to be chief guest at his own lynching party.'

'Innocent or not, my job is to uphold the law.' The marshal was adamant. 'Those folks are only scared. And you were their only way of letting off steam.'

That was no consolation to the prisoner. Again he tried urging the lawman to reconsider. 'You must know that I wouldn't shoot a man down in cold blood. That ain't my way. Farlow has it in for me because I found out. . . .'

Blake raised a hand. 'Don't matter what I think,' he averred. 'You were caught red-handed with a smoking gun in your hand and a couple of its bullets in Baz Quindle. Everybody knows there was bad blood between you.'

Even his closest ally Cody couldn't deny that things looked bad for the prisoner. 'We both know that sooner or later you and Quindle would have clashed,' Cody stressed. 'You ought to at least have given him an even break.'

Rick was lost for words. A gloomy depression settled over him. He was still trying to work out how that lowdown shyster had managed to engineer the deception. The two principal organizers of the town's defence left him alone inside the jailhouse while they went down to the barricade that had been erected across the north end of the main street.

During shooting practice that morning, Blake had been less than impressed by the wretched display of guns with which the defenders had armed themselves. Cap and ball Army Remingtons and Navy Colts predominated, together with some ancient rust-coated Springfields and a Maynard pocket pistol. One guy was even toting a single-shot Hawken long rifle.

Not exactly an armoury to stop a determined adversary like Joe McCabe, whose men would have the latest Colt revolvers and Winchester repeaters. They would have to hope and pray that the gang boss displayed a cautious approach, figuring the town was well defended. That would give him some breathing space, time to enable his meagre force to reload their old weapons.

Farlow had followed the marshal down to the barricade along with his council colleagues. And there he submitted a proposition to stop the attack. 'The council have agreed to put up five thousand dollars as an inducement for this brigand to leave Spindriff alone,' he declared, receiving the nodded support of his pathetic associates.

'It's the only way to prevent bloodshed,' Carney added. 'And we want you to go out there and parley with him.'

Blake was brutally disparaging of the proposal. 'If'n you lunkheads think that will turn a fella like Joe McCabe aside, you're pissing into the wind. He wants everything in that bank vault. And perhaps you'll recall that Rick Norton told us that he intends burning this place to the ground. And we all know the reason for that.'

'So what else can we do?' the visibly nervous town mayor stammered out.

'Go back into the church where you belong.' Blake snapped, pausing to gather himself. 'Then pray for a miracle. I'm going out there to try and reason with the critter. And say a prayer for me while you're in there. After all, I'm the one whose testimony convicted him. Maybe I can produce a rabbit out of the hat.' And with that he hitched up his gunbelt and climbed over the barricade. 'He ought to be here anytime soon.'

126

CHAPTER ELEVEN

HELL BOUND FOR SPINDRIFF

Smokin' Joe was lounging by the fire when his two spies returned to deliver their report. They were camped out five miles north of Spindriff in a narrow gulch off the main trail. Gritted teeth chewing on a dead cigar stubb greeted the two men. 'So what did you find out?' he demanded before they had even dismounted.

'Looks like it's gonna be harder than you figured, boss,' Wolf Mulligan recounted edgily. Conveying unwelcome news to the fiery gang leader was never a comfortable task. 'We went into the saloon and spun them a yarn about heading for the gold strike. They seemed to buy it.'

Weasel then took over. 'The local tin star told us about the raid they were expecting, and that they

127

weren't worried. Claimed they had plenty of men and guns to defend the town against an army.'

McCabe lit up his cigar and puffed out a couple of perfect rings as he considered this unsettling divulgence. 'Describe this jasper,' he punched out. Weasel gave a detailed depiction of his old associate, Denny Blake, the double-crossing rat who had sent him to the pen. 'So he's pinned on the tin star,' the gang boss muttered to himself. A malicious snarl cut a slash across the craggy visage.

Wolf added a further nugget of information that was equally enlightening, if not more so. 'A deputy, an old jasper well past his time . . .' He paused, ominously noting the beady twitch in McCabe's left eye.

'That has to be Saggart, the arresting officer at the trial,' was the guttural aside.

'Anyways, he asked us which way we'd come and about a place called Baxter Springs,' Maddigan continued. 'The fella seemed mighty interested as to how the trading post owner was fairing.'

McCabe knew what was coming. 'And I suppose you pair of boobies told him?' Weasel nodded unwittingly. 'You brainless clowns!' McCabe railed angrily. He jumped to his feet, grabbing the little runt and hurling him to the ground. 'I oughter plug you here and now. There ain't no trading post, never was. And Baxter died in that spot years ago. If'n you hadn't been so dumb, you'd have seen the cross where we camped last night. They'd sussed who you were. Fine pair of spies you bungling clucks turned out to be.' Mulligan backed off, not wishing to join his pal in the dust.

McCabe stamped off in a furious huff, drawing hard on the glowing cigar stub leaving his men shifting about, nervously awaiting the boss's verdict on this disquieting revelation. Stretch, who had taken over as second-in-command, exerted his new-found authority by mocking the two mugs, which helped lighten the atmosphere for the others.

Five minutes later McCabe was back, a plan of action worked out. 'Cut the squawking, you turkeys, we've got work to do.' Smokin' Joe was never one to stew over setbacks. His twisted brain was capable of quickly mutating any obstacle to his advantage. 'We'll hit the town from two sides. That should give them more than just a sore head.'

'A gut full of lead, eh boss?' Weasel cut in, fervently attempting to patch over him and his buddy's gaffe.

McCabe ignored the peace offering. That was past. Only the future mattered now. And hellfire was coming to Spindriff in the form of Smokin' Joe McCabe. 'Me, Weasel and Concho will ride in from the north to distract them. Stretch will lead you others in from the south. That way we'll trap the poor saps in a pincer movement.'

'Just like at Bull Run, boss,' interjected a mean-eyed cuss called Hambone Willis, who had been with McCabe in that brutal conflict.

McCabe responded with a meaningful nod of accord. 'And just like then, we'll come out on top.' He dug his spurs in the horse's flanks. 'OK, boys, let's go have us some fiery fun.'

Whoops and hollers unsettled a flock of quail, which fluttered skywards in panic-stricken flight as the line of riders spurred off. For most of them, it was more the hellraising before the fire for which they were most eager. The spoils of victory shared out in the form of free booze and spendable greenbacks would be the icing on the cake. Pounding hoofs echoing across the flats sounded like Indian war drums. It was music to the ears of men attuned to the forthcoming battle.

Before they rounded the thrusting promontory of Porcupine Quill on the outskirts of Spindriff, McCabe drew his men to a halt. 'We'll split up here,' he announced. 'If'n you see strong opposition on the far side,' he instructed Stretch, 'get the Wolfman here to holler out one of his coyote calls. A couple of owl hoots if, as I suspect, that claim was a big sham.'

'What are we gonna do if'n the town is too well defended, boss?' It was this glitch to their plans that had been on the minds of them all. Only Hambone had the nerve to verbalize it out loud.

McCabe had also been mulling this over in his mind. 'Reckon in that case, boys, we'll be moving on to Coronado. Rumour has it the place is wide open at the moment. This dump will be put on hold for another occasion. But sure as eggs is eggs, it'll be a temporary reprieve only.'

Stretch then departed with the bulk of their force. McCabe hung around until he was sure they had reached the far side of the town unobserved before rounding the Quill. And there was the town of

Spindriff, quiet and peaceful but for the barricade erected across the street.

Denny had heard the approaching riders before they hove into view. On seeing just three with McCabe in the lead, he stepped out from behind the barricade and walked steadfastly towards them. A hand was raised. 'Hold up there, Joe,' the Judas outlaw called out. 'Where are the rest of your men? The word is you're running more than a triple-headed gang these days.'

'Well, if'n it ain't that backstabbing varmint Mister Denny Blake himself come to welcome us into his town, boys.' The sneering crack brought terse guffaws from his two sidekicks. 'Got all that lovely dough packed up for us before we reduce you and your goddamned berg to ashes?'

Blake repeated his query. 'I guess you ain't hoping to take the town with just three men, Joe.' His searching gaze probed the terrain on either side of the scrubland. Nothing moved. 'That would be mighty foolish. We have plenty of guns to make life awful tough for you fellas.'

'Is that so?' The cynical retort was followed by a snort of derision. 'Looks to me like that barricade is manned by a heap of rusty old iron in the hands of layabouts and grave fodder.'

Blake decided to cut to the chase: 'It's me you're really after. I know that, Joe. So why don't we just have this out between the two of us? A showdown like we used to enjoy in the old days? Winner takes all. You still up for that?'

At that moment, the low yet distinct call of two owl hoots drifted on the breeze. McCabe gave no sign of having heard it, and Blake was only heedful of the gang leader's response to his challenge.

McCabe laughed at the offer. 'Now why in blue blazes should I give a treacherous turncoat like you an even break? "Winner takes all" is right. And that's gonna be me, Denny boy. Time for this confab to end.' Without warning he drew his revolver and shot the marshal dead.

The loud report was the signal for all hell to break loose. And it came from the Raiders who had come in from the far side and were now attacking the barricade. 'Okay, boys, let's give these hayseeds a lesson in real shooting.'

The defenders had been well and truly misled. Gunfire erupted from both sides of the thinly held barricade. The sudden downing of the marshal had left them hopelessly exposed, like a rudderless ship with no captain at the helm. The superior firepower of the attackers soon took its toll. Two men went down in a hail of lead.

Only the urgent cajoling of Cody Saggart enabled the townsmen to put up any form of effective resistance. 'Take careful aim. And make every shot count. Let's show these critters that Spindriff men ain't no easy pushover.'

Weasel Egger was the Raiders' first casualty, forcing McCabe to seek shelter behind some bales of hay. Concho ducked behind an abandoned buggy. Gunsmoke drifted across the battlefield. Soon two more of the defenders fell. Caught in that dreaded crablike pincer, there was little hope left for the beleaguered force. Stretch and his men pressed forwards along opposite sides of the main street. A steady barrage of lead gave the wavering defenders little chance of holding firm.

Saggart loudly cursed the spineless weaklings on the council. Brave or foolhardy, those willing to fight for the town deserved better than this. It was clear that surrender was out of the question. These braggarts were in no mood for taking prisoners. All his puny faction could do was keep firing and hope to bring some of the Raiders down before they were overwhelmed.

And that would not be long in coming. Saggart was the only defender toting a decent revolver. And he made it tell, bringing down another member of the gang from where he had sought shelter behind a water trough. But the writing was on the wall. Bullets zipped past his head. The grim hand of fate had played a macabre trick on him, for on this very spot two years before the roles had been reversed. On that occasion it had been Joe McCabe cowering behind the trough.

Cody was well aware that sticking around here would mean joining Denny Blake in the hereafter. All too soon the gun battle was over. A heavy silence descended over the defeated township. The scythe of the grim reaper had done its worst. Cody mused that he must be the sole survivor of the one-sided conflict.

And out of the grim aftermath the haunting wail

of hymn-singing from inside the church pervaded the cloying atmosphere of death. How long would it be before the invaders entered the House of God where all the women were sheltering? He shivered at the prospect of lust-hungry predators avidly sating their carnal appetites.

The ex-lawman's face was set in a determined resolve to do everything in his limited power to thwart the hideous intentions of the Arizona Raiders. And his best hope in that respect was to release the one man who could help him succeed. Red Spot Rick Norton was still locked up in the jailhouse.

Slowly he crawled beneath the raised boardwalk, making sure no noise drew any unwelcome attention. He paused as the hearty bawling of the gun-crazed aggressors drew closer. They passed his place of concealment, firing their pistols into the windows of adjacent buildings. Laughing and jostling one another they made straight for the Blue Parrot.

'After all that buckarooing,' Concho declared lustily, 'we need a few drinks to celebrate.'

'And they're all on the house, boys,' McCabe added breezily. 'These good folks won't be charging us a blamed cent.' More cheers and hoorahing as the remains of the gang stamped across the street and disappeared through the batwings. They had not come out of this unscathed, and McCabe's blood was up.

'After we've drunk this place dry,' he laughingly announced, grabbing a bottle and tipping a liberal slug down his throat, 'we'll hustle on down to the bank and pick up that dough. Then it's gonna be firework time.' More cheers and high jinx followed as guns were let off. The back mirror disappeared in a shower of glass fragments. 'Goodbye Spindriff and howdie Hellfire!'

On the far side of the street, Cody Saggart shivered. If he didn't do something the town was doomed. A few more minutes passed before he gingerly emerged from his hiding place. It was vital to ensure the gang were fully occupied in the Blue Parrot before he hastened down to the jailhouse.

CHAPTER TWELVE

TURNAROUND

The leading members of the town council stayed well hidden during the approach of the Arizona Raiders from the other direction. No chances were taken of any stray bullets heading their way. Ashen faces, grey and horror stricken, gaped at the nauseating sight of dead bodies littering the street around the barricade. Harvey Rizzlock was the first to vomit up the contents of his stomach. He was soon followed by Lem Carney. Only Judd Farlow appeared to be unaffected.

Saggart sneered at their lily-livered reaction. 'This is what comes of turning your back on the town,' he openly mocked. 'Ain't a pretty sight, is it? And there'll be more of the same if'n something isn't done to stop these murdering thugs.'

'Do you have anything in mind?' asked the contrite mayor, stroking a handkerchief across his sweating brow. Carney nodded, eager to support any form of retaliation suggested by their old lawman. 'We sure didn't expect this.' Coming face to face with the Grim Reaper in all his blood-soaked finery had shaken the pompous officials to the core. Only now were they fully able to comprehend the brutal outcome of their high-handed attitude.

'A danged pity you didn't think of that before good men had to be killed defending you.' Saggart didn't labour the point. There were more vital issues to be considered now. For the moment the Raiders had confined themselves to the Blue Parrot. But for how long? 'Far as I can see there's only one thing we can do.' The officials waited expectantly. 'I aim to set Rick Norton free. He's the only man who can help us now.'

Even with the fate of the town hanging in the balance, releasing the man they had branded a troublemaking killer was difficult to swallow. It was Farlow who voiced their reluctance. 'You certain he ain't in league with the gang?' Diffident nods of indecision followed this accusation. 'Set him free and they could team up. Then where would we be?'

The old lawdog gave the suggestion his most acerbic riposte. 'Rick Norton is worth a dozen two-faced claim jumpers like you.' He pushed the focus of his passionate resentment aside. 'Now get out of my way. I have a town to save.'

Rizzlock swallowed hard, looking at Carney for his support, then followed their retired marshal down to the jailhouse. Farlow covertly made himself scarce. His absence at the jail was overlooked by the others in the tense atmosphere. But Saggart, quickly releasing the prisoner, noted the lowlife's absence. It was pretty darned clear now that the conniving businessman had framed his buddy. 'I'm sorry to have ever doubted you, boy,' he apologized, handing the released man back his gunbelt.

Rick accepted the apology with a nod and a restrained smile as he buckled on the rig. But a dark frown hinted at murky shenanigans as he carefully examined the Colt Peacemaker. 'This isn't the gun I was carrying when Baz Quindle was shot. I took mine off'n McCabe when I escaped from his camp. That one had a bone handle.' His eyes glittered with malice. 'It proves Farlow's accusation against me was a frame-up. He was the one who pulled the trigger.'

The disclosure was a shock to the repentant officials. 'Cody ain't the only one who needs to eat some humble pie,' Rizzlock meekly admitted. 'We all need to hold our heads in shame. Can you ever forgive us, Rick? The town badly needs you to bring McCabe to heel. We'll pay you any sum you want. Ain't that so, Lem?'

'Just name your price . . . Marshal.' The banker gulped, holding out the revered tin star.

Rick accepted it with some reluctance, then stuck the badge in his pocket out of sight. His hesitation was deliberate. 'I need to think on it. As for accepting blood money, keep it. Spindriff was once my town. Now I ain't so sure.'

'It still can be, Rick, if'n you'll take the job,' Rizzlock was almost pleading. 'And I'll back you all the way against Farlow now that he's shown his true colours.'

This was neither the time nor the place for discussing the double dealings of Judd Farlow. The raucous bellowing of drunken outlaws accompanied by the constant rattle of gunfire was proof enough that Smokin' Joe and his gang were building to the horrific climax of their invasion, the total annihilation of Spindriff.

'You're jumping the gun, Mayor,' Rick cynically admonished the contrite official. He was still not prepared to forgive or forget. 'You seem to have overlooked the tricky problem of dousing McCabe's plan of robbery and destruction. He's not the kind of carbuncle you can cure with a bit of ointment.' He drew breath to make the critters sweat before grudgingly concurring. 'But I'll give it my best shot.'

An audible gasp of relief greeted the acceptance.

While he had been stuck in jail, Rick had worked out how best to lance the suppurating boil that was Joe Mccabe. The notorious gambling gunfighter's newly elected role as marshal now gave him a free rein to put the plan into action. 'Need some help, boy?' asked Saggart, joining him on the boardwalk. 'Even a roustabout like Rick Norton can't just wave the magic wand hoping those varmints will disappear into thin air.'

'Guess you're right there, partner,' the grateful saviour declared. 'I was wondering if'n an old tin star like Cody Saggart could resist a fracas like this.'

'It's in the blood, young fella.' The jaunty retort

was tempered by a stoic resolve. 'And I owe it to Denny and all those others. They may not have been on the mayor's invitation list, but their lives were forfeited for this town.'

Rick nodded as they strolled purposefully down towards the saloon. 'You get over to the hotel and keep watch from upstairs.'

'You got some'n in mind?'

Rick tapped his nose furtively. 'It's a long shot. But if'n I play this right, McCabe will fall right into the net.'

As the two friends parted, Elly Jordan appeared from a side street. She knew exactly where her ex-beau was headed. 'Don't do this, Rick. You'll only get yourself killed.' She laid a hand on his arm, the beseeching appeal contrasting markedly with her previously brittle manner. 'This town don't deserve your sympathy. We've all played you false, me included.'

'I always thought you knew me better than that, Elly.' He gently prised her hand off. 'A pity you chose to believe a rat like Farlow instead.'

'I was foolishly swayed the wrong way.' Pleading eyes earnestly sought to change his mind. 'But I realize he was only using me to further his own shady ambitions. It's you that I'm thinking of now. Please don't throw your life away.'

'Too late for that.' Nothing was going to sway him now, not even this woman whom he stilled loved with a vengeance. 'I've always been a sucker for a lost cause. Go back to the church and look after those

140

that need it. If'n my plan works, I will be able to join you there later.'

One last effort was made to dig out the truth concerning Rick's clash with her fiancé. 'At least tell me what it is you have against Judd that has put the two of you at loggerheads. And don't play the jealousy card. It doesn't wash any more.'

The tight-lipped resentment against his foe was threatening to burst out. Only a sincere concern for this woman's well-being held it in check. The sordid details had to come from the root cause of all this trouble. Nonetheless, his tone softened. 'As I told you before, Elly, you need to ask him. Then you'll understand.'

With that parting shot, he continued undaunted towards his date with destiny. But Elly Jordan was not about to let it drop. Instead of returning to the church, she hurried across the street and entered the hotel.

Cody Saggart was shocked and disturbed to hear the door open just as he was mounting the stairs to the upper storey. 'Geepers, gal!' he exclaimed, drawing his pistol. 'What you doing busting in here like that? You wanna get yourself killed?'

'I need you to tell me what Rick has against Judd,' she insisted firmly. 'I know he tells you everything. And I'm not leaving until I get at the truth.'

Like his friend, the old lawman was loath to shatter this girl's dreams. But the flinty stare pinning him to the spot brooked no deviation. He scratched his thinning head of grey hair. 'We ain't got much time so I'll make it brief.' Then with a deep sigh laden with malice, he began the sorry disclosure. 'It all started when Rick's pa refused to sell his land to Farlow. . . .'

As he strolled slowly, yet with a determined tread along the boardwalk, Rick's movements were being carefully monitored by vigilant eyes. McCabe was taking no chances of this herd of weak-kneed sheep suddenly turning into vengeful wolves. The sentinel delegated to keep watch was Wolf Maddigan. His lounging posture stiffened on spotting Red Spot Norton two blocks away. And he was heading his way.

For a man of his bulk, the Wolfman's pace was surprisingly crisp when the need arose. The boss would want to hear about this pronto. As well as Denny Blake, the removal of the Red Spot was a priority he would enjoy finalizing. McCabe was still smarting after the humiliating episode suffered at the Maricopa camp. And with the gunfighter still in Spindriff, it looked like he hadn't managed to transfer the bank dough into his own pockets.

Weaving a path behind the buildings on main street, Maddigan slipped in the rear door of the Blue Parrot. The boys were still raising Cain in the saloon bar when he entered. No preamble was needed for what he had to report: 'Red Spot is in town and he's heading down here right now.'

That news certainly caused a lull in the festivities. Every manjack there vividly recalled the gambler's wily bettering of their leader. Furtive eyes swivelled towards Smokin' Joe to observe his reaction. Tense and alert he may have been, but there were no outward signs of any anger. He topped up his glass and took another swig, dragging an arm across his lips. All he said was, 'Is he alone?'

'Nobody else in sight,' replied the lookout, 'unless you count a girl hurrying across the street.'

In the ensuing quiet, the steady rhythm of approaching boots – one set only – grew louder. They finally paused outside the saloon. 'Come on in and have a drink, Red Spot,' McCabe invited languidly. 'Today they're on the house.'

The hands of the six remaining outlaws dropped to their gun butts as Rick Norton entered the saloon. 'You're taking a big chance coming here alone,' McCabe said, pushing a filled glass across the table. 'You must know that I have to kill you. My boys would expect nothing less of their leader.' Muttered agreement as to this outcome of the meeting infiltrated the smoke-laden atmosphere.

'That would be mighty foolish, Joe,' Rick declared, sitting down. 'Seeing as we're both on the same side.' A quizzical look from the gang boss encouraged him to elucidate. 'Those critters were all for stringing me up when I returned here. They figured I was in with you. My reputation didn't help none, either.'

'So how did you escape?'

'Not everybody in Spindriff thinks Rick Norton is the Devil's spawn.'

'That don't mean nothing to me, buster,' McCabe snapped out. 'The stunt you pulled back at Maricopa deserves a reply of the terminal kind.' He drew his revolver and aimed it at the heart of his foe. Rick didn't move a muscle. 'Give me one good reason why I shouldn't pull this trigger.'

Rick smiled, lit up a cigar then applied the light to the dead stub stuck between McCabe's clenched teeth. 'I can give you twenty grand's worth.'

The outlaw's deep-set eyes widened. 'You talking about the bank dough?' The query received a curt nod. The offer was mockingly laughed down. 'What's to stop us just moseying on down there and grabbing the whole caboodle for ourselves?'

Rick shook his head. 'The good citizens of Spindriff have hidden it away. That's why.' McCabe's ugly scowl was enough to inform Rick that he had the whip hand. 'And don't figure you can take the town apart. Knowing you were coming, they sent for help. And it will be here in a couple of days.' Rick's shoulders lifted on a nonchalant shrug. 'You could strike lucky. But then again . . .' He left the dilemma hanging in the air. 'But I know exactly where it is.'

CHAPTER THIRTEEN

SUCKERED

'So what are we waiting here for?' McCabe was on his feet in a second. 'Lead the way, Red Spot, and we'll follow close behind.'

'And you gun me down in the back?' Rick scoffed. 'I ain't falling for that one, Joe.' His face was set in stone. 'We do this my way, or not at all. And we split the proceeds right down the middle.' It was a blunt-edged proposition without any menace. A defiant gaze, solid and unyielding, intimated that Joe McCabe had no other choice. And he was right. 'Is it a deal?'

Tension a sharp knife would be hard pressed to chop asunder gripped the reduced gathering of owl-hoots. Rick knew he was walking a tightrope as he waited on McCabe's response. The gang leader chewed on his glowing cigar, mulling over the ulti-matum. The slightest wrong move on Rick's part

145

could precipitate a gun battle from which he had no chance of emerging in one piece. But he was counting on greed winning the stand-off in his favour. He could almost hear the wheels turning inside McCabe bullet head as he considered the limited options.

'This town has cost me dear, mister,' McCabe grumbled. 'And that's down to your warning them of our intentions. I ought to kill you right here and now.' Six other guns backed up the threat. Rick remained stock still, a statue hewn from granite. 'But ten grand is better than nothing. What's your play?'

A collective whoosh issued from dry throats as the tension palpably eased. Rick released a deep sigh, suddenly aware that he also had been holding his breath. 'Two of your boys come along to make sure I'm on the level,' he said, enthused that his plan to snare the gang was being put into operation. 'The rest of you wait here. Soon as you get the nod, follow on. I'll take my cut and disappear afore you arrive. Not that I don't trust you, Joe.' A cynical grin split the handsome face.

'Just make certain you don't take it all. We have a deal, remember?' McCabe held out a hand ostensibly to clinch the agreement.

Rick ignored the gesture. He would rather trust a snake in his bed. Although he kept that view strictly to himself. 'These rannies will make sure I play fair.'

McCabe shrugged off the snub. It didn't matter none. He was satisfied with the arrangement. Just so long as that dough was forthcoming, what was a handshake? 'Wolf and Jumbo. You rannies make sure he don't pull any tricks.'

Stifling a smile of approval, Rick led the way down the street, crossing over to the hotel. Concho was also watching from the saloon door. 'Where have they gone?' demanded the surly voice of Joe McCabe.

'Looks like the dough is hidden inside the hotel,' was the animated reply. The three men were heading directly for the National. Rick entered by the front door, striding purposefully round behind the reception desk, now unoccupied. The desk clerk had long since vacated his post, preferring the dubious safety offered by the church. The two delegated guardians followed Rick's every movement as they moved in behind him. Avaricious imaginations were conjuring up all manner of profligate entertainment their cut would fulfil.

Accordingly, they failed to heed the lurking figure watching their progress from the head of the stairs. Cody Saggart had quickly cottoned on to Rick's plan of action when he spotted the three men emerging from the Blue Parrot. Time slipped away as old habits slotted effortlessly into place.

After relating the sordid details of Judd Farlow's unscrupulous acquisition of the Norton holding and Chester's death, Cody had commiserated with the distraught girl. 'Don't be too hard on yourself, Elly,' he sympathized. A kindly hand was placed on her shoulder. 'The devious skunk had us all fooled. It ain't no wonder that he's disappeared.' He then saw her out of the back door, anticipating that she would

147

return to the church.

Down in the lobby, Rick pointed into the darkened recess. 'The money is in some saddle-bags hidden in that closet.' The two men hesitated, not sure if the renowned gambler was playing them false. Rick held his hands up, addressing the sneering bulk of Jumbo who was still smarting from his besting back in the Maricopa. 'I'll stay back here with Wolf while you take a look-see.'

Jumbo was still not entirely convinced. He hesitated, seeking his sidekick's approval. 'What do you reckon, Wolf? Is this rat on the level?'

'Only one way to find out,' Wolf urged. 'No sense in hanging around. And the boss'll get twitchy if'n we don't hurry.'

Jumbo cautiously moved across the lobby and behind the desk. He pulled open the door and peered inside the closet. Although Wolf's avaricious gaze was drawn to the actions of his associate, he was astute enough to keep his eye on their unwelcome partner. 'Is there anything in there?' he rasped out.

'Looks like Red Spot was telling the truth,' Jumbo excitedly replied. 'I can see a pair of bulging saddlebags.' In effect, what he had discovered was the property of the would-be assassin, Hatchet Mag Luffrey, who was now a permanent resident in the abandoned Cleopatra Mine outside Spindriff. Rick had deposited them in the closet himself when the desk clerk was temporarily absent. Now, they provided a fitting lure that had worked a treat.

Wolf pushed Rick in front of him, eager to feast his

148

own peepers on the loot. That was when both men received a shock they could never have dreamed up: Cody Saggart appeared at the top of the stairs brandishing his revolver. 'Raise your hands!' he rapped out, slowly descending the staircase. 'One false move and you're both grave fodder.' The jabbing six-gun backed up by Rick was enough encouragement to prevent any wayward acts of bravado.

'Tie them up with this,' Rick told his buddy, handing over a coil of rope. His own hogleg ensured no resistance was attempted by the bewildered outlaws. 'Then stick these jaspers on the bottom step where they can be seen from the door.'

Jumbo was seething that once again he had been fooled. That said, he had no option but to concede defeat without a murmur. But Wolf Maddigan was not so crestfallen, and voiced his reply with the aggressive posture of his namesake. 'You won't get away with this, Red Spot,' he growled. 'Smokin' Joe is bound to smell a rat and come looking for us.'

Rick hawked out a mocking guffaw. 'That's exactly what I want, dummy. Now shut your trap!' Just to make sure no warning was given by the truculent captives, he gagged both men firmly with their own bandannas. 'Now we wait.'

Rick commandeered one of the outlaw pistols as both men took up their positions, himself being at the head of the stairs, with his buddy concealed in an alcove to one side of the lobby. And they didn't have long to hang around. McCabe was impatient to secure the reward and eager to finish the job of renaming the town 'Hellfire'. Rick watched him stamping across the street, leading the rest of his men.

The outlaw's warped snarl boded ill for any skulduggery encountered. He lumbered to a halt in the open doorway of the hotel on witnessing the duo of tethered prisoners staring back at him. A rabid curse burst forth as he assumed the worst. 'That two-timing double crosser has lit out with all the dough,' he rasped, exasperated with himself as much as the alleged thief for agreeing to the skunk's proposition. Smokin' Joe had been suckered once again, and it hurt.

The empty saddle-bags stuck in the middle of the lobby appeared to prove the conjecture. It was unfortunate that the blustering gang boss failed to notice the warning signs emanating from the animated features of Wolf Maddigan. Never one to lie down and cry over split milk, McCabe quickly ordered two of his men to untie the prisoners. 'Me and the rest will get the horses,' he was already turning round and heading back to the saloon. 'He must have headed south, hoping to reach the border. Otherwise we'd have spotted the rat riding past the Blue Parrot.'

It was a piece of panic-stricken logic, ignoring the fact that numerous other routes out of Spindriff were available. Stretch and an ex-slave called Blackbird were berating the gullibility of the prisoners none too gently when Rick ordered them to back off. 'Drop your gunbelts, pronto. Then we'll add you pair of numbskulls to the heap of garbage.' The two men froze, unable to absorb what was happening. Saggart stepped out from his place of concealment, adding his weight to the order.

Unfortunately neither of the two schemers had reckoned on McCabe leaving a man to keep guard outside the hotel. Concho was about to shoot the unsuspecting new marshal when out of the corner of his eye he spotted Cody Saggart emerging from cover. It was a kneejerk reaction that made him swing the Manhatten .36 Navy towards the nearby threat. The gun barked, driving the old-timer back with a bullet in his shoulder – not a killing shot, but enough to terminate any further involvement of the ex-lawdog in the deadly conflict.

Had Concho made a more rational evaluation, he would have removed the main danger on the stairs. The misjudgement gave Rick time to trigger off a couple of shots towards the window. Concho ducked out of sight. The unwelcome diversion gave the two rescuing outlaws a chance to draw their own weapons. But they weren't fast enough to prevent the slick gunfighter clipping the Blackbird's wings. A second shot finished him off permanently.

Stretch took advantage of his black sidekick's demise to dive behind a large stuffed chair, from which he returned fire. One bullet sliced through Rick's left arm, a stinging reminder that he was up against desperate men who would stop at nothing to achieve their violent ends. He turned side on behind a wooden pillar, firing his remaining bullets at the hidden adversary. Holstering the empty revolver, he quickly palmed the appropriated Cooper five-shot, hoping it would be enough to finish the mêlée in his favour.

Only a single shot was fired in reply from the concealed brigand. Rick smiled. The jasper had clearly not reloaded after all the celebratory shooting in the Blue Parrot. Stretch was well aware of the peril he faced. He struggled to manhandle the chair backwards towards the door, hoping to join Concho. But the unwieldy piece of furniture was too heavy to drag more than a few inches at a time. Taking his chances, the brigand leapt to his feet and made a dash for the open door.

He would have made it had he not tripped over one of his tethered buddies. Two .36 calibre shells drilled into his exposed torso. The odds were slowly but surely shifting in favour of Red Spot Rick. He hurried down the stairs to check on Cody. 'The bullet went straight through. I'll be all right,' his pal replied, although obviously in a lot of pain. Rick untied his bandanna and strapped up the wound. 'Go finish this off, pal,' Cody urged. 'You've gotten the critters running scared.'

Rick was none too sure of that, but responded with an optimistic nod before turning to continue the fight. He mounted the stairs and hurried to the end of the corridor. There he gingerly emerged on to the veranda facing the main street.

Over on the far side he could see Concho sheltering behind the water trough. The rannie was waiting for him to come out of the front door. He needed something to lure him out into the open. McCabe was nowhere to be seen. The wily critter was doubtless biding his time to mount an ambush of his own. So Rick needed to be extra careful about tackling Concho.

The empty revolver stuck in his holster provided the answer. Flinging it over to his left, the weapon bounced on the overhanging boardwalk canopy of the adjacent premises, which happened to be a saddlery. The loud clatter was enough for the hidden owlhoot to figure his quarry was attempting to outflank him.

Concho yelled out to the unseen Joe McCabe. 'He's in the tack store, boss. It's only single storey and separate from the others. We've gotten the bastard trapped.' Keyed up to fever pitch and reckless following all the drinking and shooting, Concho leapt to his feet. All sense of caution had gone to the wind. His aim was to reach the side of the building adjacent to the hotel. 'I'll keep him busy from this side,' he hollered. Those were to be his last words.

The whole attention of the unwitting villain was focused on the store. Half way across the street, a brittle order, measured yet venomous, heralded his departure from this mortal coil. 'Too late, Concho. The Reaper's called your name.'

No chance to surrender was offered. This battle was now an all-or-nothing confrontation. Two shots rang out, both dead centre in the outlaw's chest. Concho was stopped in his tracks. Before his body had hit the dirt, Rick had dashed to the far end of the veranda and down the access steps to ground level.

Flattened against the side of the hotel, he made his final challenge: 'It's just you and me now, Joe.' The shouted summons to mortal combat echoed across the empty street. Carried on the wind, he had no doubt that McCabe would have heard it. The deathly climax to the brutal invasion was approaching its zenith. And only one man would walk away from the encounter. Rick could only pray that he would not be occupying that vacant hole in the cemetery any time soon.

Only after issuing the brazen challenge to his unseen opponent did the realization hit his highly charged brain that any real means of coming out of the confrontation on top was sadly lacking. The gun held in his hand was also now empty. Not only that, it was an old percussion pistol – so no help from his shell belt, which contained .45 calibre bullets. He cursed his folly in rashly tossing away his weapon of choice. Now unarmed, he would need to secure a shooter quickly if he was to emerge victorious from this life or death struggle.

CHAPTER
FOURTEEN

THE DIE IS CAST

It was Cody Saggart who came to his aid. The old-timer had dragged himself to the front window of the hotel, where he spotted his pal hiding in the doorway of the adjoining saddlery. Rick's dilemma was obvious. 'Take this, buddy,' he whispered, passing his own Peacemaker through the window. 'It's fully loaded. You're gonna need something better than that old Cooper.'

'Much obliged.' Rick gratefully took charge of the much revered equalizer. The single-action Colt .45 with its brass cartridges possessed the balance, reliability and feel preferred by all those who needed the protection of an accurate firearm.

Originally produced for peace officers only, hence its nickname, the revolver was quick to load and soon came to symbolize the wild heyday of the American frontier.

'Take care, buddy,' Cody advised his friend. 'That critter ain't escaped the law this long through being careless. He's got more lives than a cat.'

'Well, this'll be his last one. Now you go find Doc Pilger and get that wound fixed,' Rick exhorted his friend. A wave of the hand and he disappeared down a nearby alley. He did not have long to experience the warning issued by his pal.

A shot fired from the livery stable clipped the woodwork inches from his head. Splinters of flying wood tickled his cheek, drawing more blood. He winced, ducking down behind a wagon. Peering around the edge of the raised sides, he tried to determine the exact location of his adversary. Two more slugs ricocheted off the steel-rimmed wheels.

The wagon was stuck out in the open on a back lot behind the main street. McCabe was secreted in the hay loft of the stable, where a loading bay enabled him to effectively cover the ground outside. Rick pumped a couple of shots at the opening to keep the skunk's head down. The distraction allowed him time to dart across the open corral to the edge of the barn. He eased inside, dodging into an empty stall.

And there he paused, ears attuned for the slightest movement overhead. Nothing. McCabe was lying doggo. More time passed, each man waiting for the other to make a false move. It was Rick who decided to bring the unwholesome stalemate to its grisly conclusion. 'This ain't getting us nowhere, Joe,' he called out. 'What say we have it out man-to-man?'

For what seemed like an hour, in effect no more than a minute, there was no answer. Only the gentle snicker of a horse in the adjoining stall disturbed the silence. Had the varmint skedaddled? Rick echoed his previous challenge, adding a mocking taunt. 'Maybe the reputation you've acquired is like that butt stuck in your mouth, all smoke and no fire.'

The biting insult secured the desired outcome. A gruff voice, tetchy yet doggedly resolute, filtered down through the upper floorboards. 'You after a shoot-out, Red Spot? Then you've gotten your wish.' A macabre laugh followed. 'Denny Blake made the same fatal mistake. But more to the point, how do I secure the dough once you've been removed from the picture?' Confidence of emerging the winner oozed from the cocky braggart's reply.

'If by some lucky chance you beat me to the draw, the town will be in your hands, Joe. Lem Carney is the bank manager. Just offer him your usual friendly greeting and he'll be putty in your hands.'

'OK, it's a deal. We meet out front of the stable in two minutes. You from one side, me from the other. Agreed?'

'I'll be waiting, Joe. And I've got eyes like a hawk, so no tricks.' There was no reply, only a shuffling as the leader of the now defunct Arizona Raiders carefully descended the ladder at the far end of the stable. Rick was waiting near the open door when he came into view around the far end.

Both men were displaying caution as they stepped

157

away from the wooden walls. Clawed hands hovered above gun butts in readiness for the age-old duel to the finish. It was McCabe who spoke first. He was looking beyond his opponent. 'Seems like there's two of us who want you out the way, Red Spot.' A languid hand indicated that an unseen assailant was lurking behind where Rick was standing. 'And he's holding a shotgun.'

'I ain't falling for that old trick,' Rick scoffed. 'Now fill your hand and let's get this over with.'

'Suit yourself, buddy. Looks like I can't lose.' McCabe couldn't resist a vigorous chortle. 'Get ready to meet your Maker.'

As one, both men reached for their guns. In such situations, Rick had managed to perfect the reflex action of leaning to his left while his right hand palmed the revolver. The triumphant manoeuvre made him a trifle slower on the draw. But of far more significance, it gave him a winning hand. A bullet from McCabe's revolver zipped past where his head had been moments before. Two shots triggered from the borrowed Peacemaker were far more deadly, ploughing into the villain's ribcage. McCabe lurched backwards. His mouth dropped open as the realization came that once again this jasper had suckered him. And this time for keeps. No more lives for Joe McCabe to call on. The Reaper's invitation was final.

Rick stood where he was, hands falling to his side. And that was when the echo of a second shot bounced off the walls of the livery barn. And it had come from behind where he was standing. He spun round, sinking to one knee. Judd Farlow stood there, the unfired shotgun at his feet. Blood was pouring from an arm wound. The other was reaching for his revolver when a second shot finished him off.

And standing behind him was Elly Jordan. She threw the Remington-Beals pocket revolver to one side as if it were a snake. Tears welled in her eyes as she suddenly appreciated that she had taken a human life. Swaying erratically as dizziness threatened to overwhelm her, she would have fallen had not Rick scooted across to support her.

That was when the floodgates opened. She clung desperately in the strong arms of her old flame. 'I never thought he'd stoop that low,' she sobbed. Rick held her tight, gently stroking her hair. 'I had to do it. There was no other choice. He would have killed you.'

'I know, honey,' he whispered. 'He had it coming. Nobody can hold it against you.' More cajoling and caressing followed as Rick Norton eased his one true love back into some sense of normality, if that feeling could ever be retrieved.

'How could I have been such a fool to be taken in by that evil charlatan?' Now secretly enjoying the girl's closeness as the townsfolk gathered around adding their congratulations, Rick made no attempt to answer questions. More to the point, nor did he acknowledge the numerous apologies from people who, earlier in the day, were all set to string him up.

Slowly with a measured tread, he guided Elly back to her buggy, helping her up on to the bench seat.

He then climbed up beside her and threw down the tin star at the feet of Harvey Rizzlock. 'You folks are going to need a new lawman,' he remarked in a flat monotone devoid of emotion. 'But it sure won't be me. Perhaps you can persuade Cody Saggart to resume his old job.' The warm smile was solely for his patched-up buddy who was standing outside the jail.

Then without a word to the contrite citizens, he whipped up the team and rode away. Once they were out of town, he sought to pose the very same proposition he had put to Elly on his return to Spindriff. His mouth opened, yet still he hesitated. She had saved his life. But was that all it was? Prevention of a heinous crime. Or did she still harbour feelings towards him? Those self-same passions of love that had never deserted him during their forced separation. 'I need to know . . . whether or not. . . .' Afraid to receive another rejection, his voice trailed off.

Elly sensed what was churning round inside his head. 'If you're about to propose what I think you are – and I sincerely hope it is a proposal – then the answer is an emphatic yes on both counts!'

Rick was stumped for words. He drew the buggy to a halt. And with a family of gophers looking on, kissed her passionately on the lips. She responded with genuine ardour. The chirruping of the small creatures appeared to be a resounding approval that life was going to be an idyllic dream come true raising oranges and more in California.